Do a ZOOMdo

Do a

™ do

Edited by Bernice Chesler

Little, Brown and Company
Boston-Toronto

Studio photography by Bliss Bruen.
Line illustrations by Peggy Adler.
ZOOMdoer photography by Jack Shipley.
Additional illustrations by Gene Mackles, Janet Krause, Karen Foote Richards.

Design by Barbara Bell Pitnof

LIBRARY OF CONGRESS CATALOGING IN PUBLICATION DATA

Main entry under title:

Do a ZOOMdo

    From the viewers of the television series ZOOM
    Includes index.
    SUMMARY: Instructions for making toys, games, jewelry, and many other items from easily available materials.
    1. Handicraft — Juvenile literature. 2. Toy making — Juvenile literature. 3. Games — Juvenile literature.
[1. Handicraft. 2. Toy making. 3. Games]
I. Chesler, Bernice. II. ZOOM
TT160.D6   745.59   75-19307
ISBN 0-316-98801-4

ISBN 0-316-98800-6 (pbk.)

ZOOM was created by Christopher Sarson.

BP

Published simultaneously in Canada by Little, Brown & Company (Canada) Limited

Printed in the United States of America

Dedicated to

D. Keith Carlson

who, for four years
as a ZOOMdo and ZOOMguest producer
and as a studio director,
fashioned the ideas of children
into the television programs
that made this book possible.

With love and thanks.

The ZOOMstaff

Dear ZOOMviewers:

This book is a result of the television series that you have helped create. For four years the ZOOMers have said, "We need you" and "Send it to ZOOM." You have responded with more than 1.5 million letters full of ideas for plays, illustrated stories, jokes, games, and do's; in short, everything that ZOOM is. Television programs do not often ask people to do anything at home or to play a creative role in building the program, so all of us at ZOOM are very pleased and inspired by the extent that you have wanted to "give it a try."

If ZOOM means any one thing, it means "you, too, can do something."

We are very happy that *Do a ZOOMdo* represents so well this spirit of ZOOM. You have seen on the air some of the do's. Some, because we get more ideas than we can use, have never been on the programs.

So enjoy these do's. Happy viewing. And thank you.

Austin Hoyt
Executive Producer

Contents

BOAT

When John lived on a small island off the coast of Portugal he used to look out his window and see ships sailing on the ocean.

You will need:

> a piece of heavy cardboard (about 3 feet by 4 feet)
> pencil
> scissors
> construction paper
> glue
> Popsicle sticks or matches
> 3 three-foot wooden dowels (thin wooden rods)
> thin, short pieces of wood
> knife
> solid-color cloth
> string

Here's what you do:

1. Fold the large piece of cardboard in half.
2. Draw a boat on the cardboard so that the fold in the cardboard is the bottom of the boat.
3. Cut out the boat shape.
4. Fold a piece of construction paper and cut two pieces to fit on the ends of the boat.
5. Glue them to the boat on each end to close the open ends.
6. Cut out a piece of cardboard that will fit into the top of the boat for the deck.
7. Make three holes in the deck for masts.
8. Glue the deck onto the boat.
9. Glue the Popsicle sticks one by one onto out-

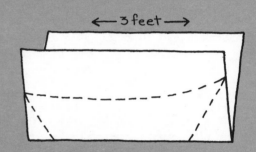

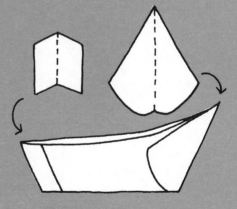

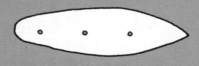

side of the boat and on the deck. Completely cover all the cardboard.

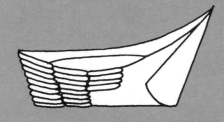

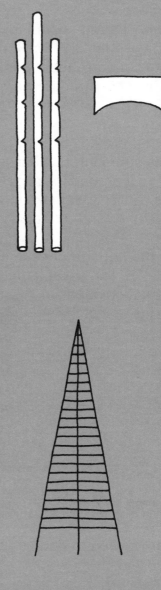

10. If you want cabins on your boat, make them out of construction paper and glue them onto the deck between the mast holes.

11. The three dowels are used for the masts which will hold up the sails. Cut a little off two dowels so that you have one three-foot dowel which will be the center mast.

12. Cut three notches into each dowel. Glue thin pieces of wood into the notches.

13. Cut out three sails for each dowel piece that is being used as a mast. Use any kind of solid-color cloth.

14. Glue sails to the three pieces of wood in each mast.

15. Put masts into holes in deck. The longest mast should go in the middle. Push the masts in until they touch the bottom of the boat and then put some glue around the dowels near the deck to hold the masts in place.

16. Each mast needs a ladder. For each ladder cut three pieces of string a little longer than the length of the exposed mast. Glue the three strings together at one end. Now cut short pieces of string for the rungs and glue them vertically up the ladder (from the middle string to the two end strings).

17. Glue the top of each ladder to the top of each mast and then glue the bottom of the ladder to the deck.

18. Now you have a boat!

ZOOMdoer: John DeSilva
Cambridge, Massachusetts

Homemade Yo-Yo

You will need:
  an empty thread-spool 1 inch long
  a piece of string 2½ feet long
  2 small cottage cheese lids
  1 piece of construction paper (optional)
  tacks

Here's what you do:
1. Put the string through the spool.
2. Then tie it around the spool and tie it again tightly at the center so it looks like the picture.
3. At the other end of the string, tie a loop for your finger.
4. Tack the cottage cheese lids to the ends of the spool. You can cover them with circles of colored construction paper.
5. Wrap the rest of the string around the spool.

You have a homemade yo-yo that should look like the drawing.

— Sharon Bernsen
Westwood, Massachusetts

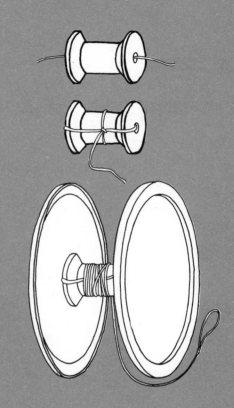

A Firildak

My father learned to do this as a boy in Turkey. He taught me and I'll show you.

You will need:
  a nail
  a hammer
  a piece of wood 1 foot long and 3 inches wide
  string that is 3 feet long

Here's what you do:
1. Put a hole in the center near a 3-inch end of the wood.
2. Put the string into the hole and make a knot near the piece of wood.
3. Have your friends stand away.
4. Give the wood a twirl before you spin it over your head.

— Feza Koprucu
Winchester, Massachusetts

Button-in-the-Cup

I have a game I make at home. To make it,

You will need:
  string
  clothespin
  one button
  a tack
  egg carton

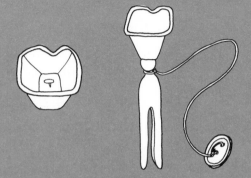

Here's what you do:
1. Tie the string around the clothespin.
2. Then tie the button on the other end of the string.
3. With a tack put a piece of your egg carton on top of the clothespin.
4. Now try to get the button in the cup.

— Sheila Tansey
Toledo, Ohio

God's Eyes

You will need:
  2 straws or sticks
  colored yarn

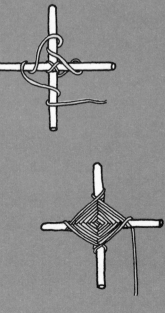

Here's what you do:
1. For the base you can use the two straws or sticks. Tie them together at the center with colored yarn.
2. Working from the center, loop the yarn around one arm of the cross and then keep going in the same direction and loop the yarn around each arm in turn.
3. Keep the yarn tight. As each row is completed, push the yarn down toward the center and just keep going.
4. If you want to change the color, tie the two yarns together, making sure that the knot goes to the back of the *God's Eye,* so it won't be seen in front of the design.
5. To finish the *God's Eye,* tie the end of the yarn to one of the sticks.

— Renee Hernendez
Orange, New Jersey

Dear ZOOM:

Enclosed in this letter I have a poem about a sled. Most of the poem is true, except for the last part because it hasn't snowed yet in Baltimore this year. I want to tell you the true story of the sled my friend, Sara Poeztch (pronounced "Petch") and I built. All of the sled is made out of wood. Sara's mother helped us build it. We got a five-foot by two-foot board to use as the main part (the part you sit on) and two four-foot by six-inch boards as the runners. After we nailed it together, Sara's mother curved the runners* for us. We wanted to paint the sled black and white like a penguin, but we only had pink paint, so we painted the sled pink. Sara had a lot of cardboard polka dots, so we stuck them on too. Then we varnished it and waxed the runners. We decided to call the sled the "Pink Pussycat."

Your friend,
Sandy Bernstein
Baltimore, Maryland

P.S. Our sled has no steering.

* 1. SLED RUNNERS

2. "CURVED SLED RUNNERS

The Wooden Sled

One spring day, two girls they said
"I think we should try to build a sled."
You can give those girls some praise,
for they finished that sled in a couple of days.

Because the winter was far ahead,
in the cellar was kept the sled.
At last the summer did come and go,
but it seemed as the northwind just wouldn't blow.

Then it happened one day at last,
when it started to snow and accumulate fast.
So they took the sled to the nearest hill,
but it wouldn't go, it just stood still.

And that was the end of their wooden sled,
but the girls weren't sad, they were happy instead.
For in the cellar that very next day,
their mother has worked, and worked away.
When she came up she looked half dead,
Saying, "Well, girls, I built you a sled!"

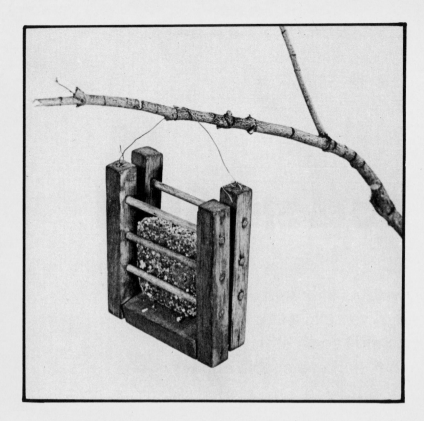

Wooden Bird Feeder

You will need:
    wood board — ¾ inch thick x 14½ inches long x
      1¾ inches wide
    ruler
    pencil
    saw (small)
    ¼ inch dowel —- 30 inches long
    drill (¼ inch bit)
    sandpaper (medium)
    hammer
    six 1¼ inch nails
    paint brush
    stain and shellac
    wire

Here's what you do:
1. From your ¾ inch thick board cut:
    — 4 pieces, each ¾ inch wide and 5½ inches
      long, for the sides of the feeder

> — 1 piece, 1¾ inches wide and 3½ inches long for the base

2. Now cut 6 pieces from the dowel, each 5 inches long.

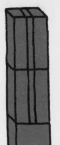

This is the way to cut up your piece of wood.

3. Sand all 11 pieces until they are smooth.
4. Drill three ¼-inch holes in each of the 4 sides:
   > — the first hole should be 1 inch down from the top;
   >
   > — the second hole should be 1 inch down from the first hole;
   >
   > — the third hole should be 1 inch down from the second hole.

5. Sand the inside of each hole using a nail with sandpaper wrapped around it.
6. Press fit the dowels into the holes between the two sides.
7. Nail sides to the base with 4 nails.

   Two sides should go on one end of the base and the other two sides on the other end, with sides opposite each other connected by the dowels.

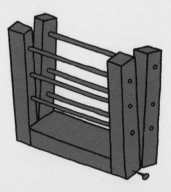

8. Nail the other 2 nails on the top of the two sides diagonally across from each other.

   Bend the nails over to make hooks for the wire.
9. Stain the bird feeder a natural wood color. Wipe the excess off and let it dry overnight.

   When it's dry, shellac with clear shellac so that the bird feeder will be waterproof.
10. Find a place to hang the bird feeder.

   A sheltered window under the eaves would be a good place if it's near trees. Hang it with wire. The feeder should be easy to fill and hard for the squirrels to eat from.

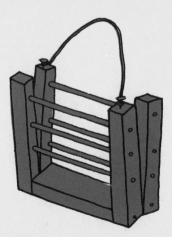

11. For bird food use a sandwich of beef suet, seeds, grain, or even peanut butter.

The best time to attract birds is in the fall.

> — Charlie Durham
> North Reading, Massachusetts

Buttonhole Puzzle

You will need:
    Popsicle stick
    drill (or a sharp, pointed object)
    string
    sweater or shirt

Here's what you do:

1. First make a small hole in one end of the stick.

2. Thread a loop of string through it, making the loop just a bit too short to go over the other end of the stick.
3. Tie and then put glue on the knot.
4. Use a sweater or soft shirt with large buttonholes (the puzzle works best if you use a buttonhole that's near a corner of the material). Place the loop of string around the corner of fabric and the buttonhole and then poke the free end of the stick through the buttonhole.

Now, can you get it off?

ZOOMdoer: Tammy Coffin
Sudbury, Massachusetts

Cups Puzzle

Put two cups upside down and one cup right side up.
Now, moving two cups at a time, get them all upside down or right side up in three tries.

— Caryn Bitgood
Danbury, Connecticut

a   b   c

Answer on page 112.

Paper Circles Picture

You will need:
   construction paper in a variety of colors (You could try using other paper that is not too thin.)
   a paper hole puncher (If you can find two that punch different sizes, your picture may be more interesting.)
   glue

Here's what you do:
1. Draw a picture on a piece of paper that is a different color than the paper you will use for the holes you will punch.
2. Punch out many holes from the other pieces of paper.
3. Glue the circles into place on the design you drew. Half cover some of them as you go along.

It's slow work. Enjoy the final picture.

— Kathie Gimla
Hoffman Estates, Illinois

Paper Cup Puppets

You will need:
- paper cup
- buttons or beads
- glue
- felt marker
- paper strips
- piece of cloth

Here's what you do:

1. Make a hole in the side of the cup. (This will be the nose. Be sure it is big enough for your finger to fit through.)

2. Glue buttons or beads onto the cup to form a face. You could draw the face. Sometimes it is better if you rub the cup with a soapy cloth, let dry and then use the felt marker.

3. Glue on the paper strips to make hair.

4. Make three holes in the cloth — big enough for your thumb, pointer and little fingers to fit through.

5. Put the cloth on your hand and put your pointer finger through the cloth up into the nose hole in the cup. Your thumb and little finger will be the puppet's "hands."

— Patrick Lugo, Brentwood, New York
Cathy Glatzel, New Milford, Pennsylvania

There are other things you can use for the head.
A hollow rubber ball is suggested by Jack Pickell, Beverly, Massachusetts.
Mike Campeta of Valatie, New York, uses a ping pong ball.

Spiral-Go-Round

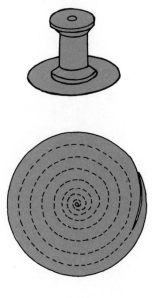

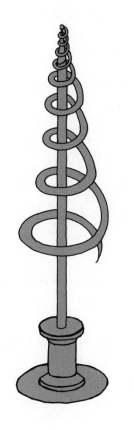

You will need:

- 1 large empty spool
- a round piece of cardboard about 2 inches in diameter
- paints
- brushes
- small piece of bright colored construction paper
- scissors
- compass with pencil
- new, just-sharpened pencil
- glue

Here's what you do:

1. Glue the spool to the center of the cardboard circle. This will be the base.
2. Paint the base and let it dry.
3. Cut out a circle from the construction paper 3 inches in diameter. (Set the compass to 1½ inch radius. Don't make a hole with the compass point. There should be a slight indentation in the center of the paper circle — not a hole.)
4. Cut paper circle into a spiral.
   Begin cutting on the side that does not have the depression in it.
   Cut around and around making a continuous spiral from the outer edge almost to the center.
   Leave a little circle in the center.
5. Push pencil down into spool with the sharp end sticking up.
6. Place the paper spiral on the pencil so that the point rests in the depression.
7. To make it go around put it on a radiator or close to a base board refrigerator or near a hot air register.

— Cynthia Primus
Dorchester, Massachusetts

SALT PENDULUM

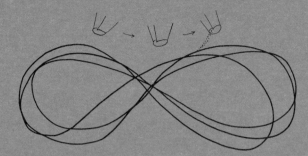

This pattern will happen right before your eyes.

To make it happen:

1. Make a cone of paper (you could use a funnel). String it up in a doorway, using tape.
2. Place black paper on the floor across the doorway.

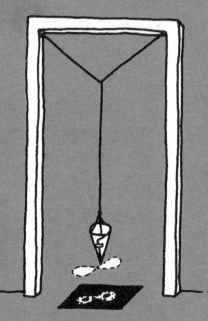

3. Pinch the bottom of the cone together, and have a friend pour salt into it. Now let the pendulum go. It will swing for a while and make geometric figures.

puppet

You will need:
   a square piece of paper
   crayons

Here's what you do:

1. Make two diagonal creases in your paper and open it up so that it looks like this:

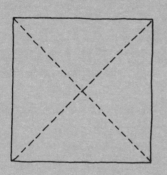

2. Fold all 4 corners so that all 4 points are touching in the center.
3. Flip the paper over.
4. Again, fold all 4 corners so that all 4 points are touching on the center.

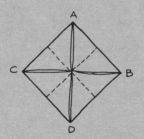

5. Fold A to B, C to D. Crease, then unfold.

6. Fold A to C, B to D. Crease, then unfold.
7. Flip the paper over.
   There should be 4 pockets.
   Slip your thumb and forefingers into these pockets.
   Pinch fingers and thumb together.
   By moving your fingers up and down, you can make your puppet talk.

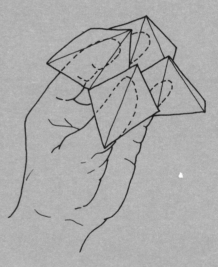

8. Using crayons or a pen, draw eyes and nose on the outside. You could open the "mouth" and draw tongue and teeth.

Some ZOOMers play a fortune-telling game with this puppet head.

— Jo Ellen Parker
Derby, Kansas

Dear ZOOM:

I watch you every day. And I am going to tell you how to make a *Humbuzzer.*

You will need:
    a tube that comes from paper towels
    a piece of waxed paper
    a rubber band
    a pencil

Here's what you do:
1. Take the tube and put a piece of waxed paper over one end.
2. Then put the rubber band over the waxed paper to hold it down.
3. Then take a pencil and poke holes in the waxed paper.
4. Hum into the end where there is no waxed paper.

Try it!

Sincerely,

Karen Cicotte (see-Cat)
Mtn. Home A.F.B. Idaho

Paper Copter

You will need:
    paper, one piece 8½ x 11 inches (regular size)
    scissors
    paper clips

Here's what you do:
1. Fold the paper in half.

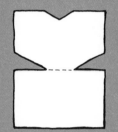

2. At the top and halfway down each side of the paper cut out 3 triangles.

3. On the top half cut in the middle as far as the fold.
4. Snip in a little further from the side triangles and fold the bottom sides to the middle and secure with 1 large or 2 small paper clips.

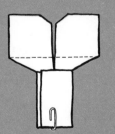

5. Fold the flaps along the dotted line, folding one flap forward and one flap back.

— Erik Petersen
St. Thomas, U.S. Virgin Islands

Toss it in the air and watch it spin down!

Beads and Things

To make paper beads you will need:
    a colorful magazine page
    scissors
    toothpick
    glue
    needle
    thread
    shellac

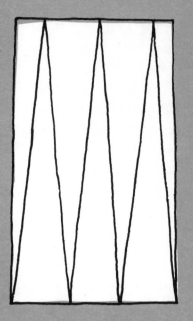

Here's what you do:
1. Placing the magazine page widthwise, measure and mark off 1-inch marks along the bottom. On the top, start with a half-inch mark and then do 1-inch marks the rest of the way.
   Connect the marks so that your lines look like the drawing.
2. Cut along all the lines.
3. Roll the pieces of paper tightly around a toothpick, starting at the wider end of the paper.
4. Dab some glue on the end when it is all rolled up.
5. Press gently to make sure the end stays.
6. Wait until the glue is dry, remove the toothpick, and go on rolling the next bead.
7. String them together to make a necklace or bracelet.
8. Dip the strung beads in shellac and let dry.

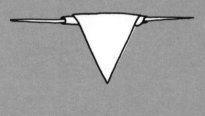

If you want to combine them with small nuts and berries you could make a *Nature Necklace*. In that case use fishline instead of thread and a needle large enough to thread fishline.

— Todd Schoeider
Kitchener, Ontario

Michele Carty of Poughkeepsie, New York, makes a different kind of bead *by cutting the paper* into pieces about 1 inch wide and 2½ inches long:
    — Hold a piece vertically and put a thin line of glue at the top.
    — Then roll it over into a tube letting the glue stick the edges together.
    — Make as many of these as you can fit on the string.

Snippings Art

To make your own snippings art you will need:
    paper (maybe one piece that is 12 x 12 inches)
    scissors
    glue
    crayons (or pen)
    a piece of paper (possibly colored) for snipping

Here's what you do:
1. Cut into the paper randomly.
2. Look at the pieces and if some look like something to you, glue them onto a piece of paper.
3. You can color them or draw on them.

Elf's shoe

bird flying

pen in an inkwell

Paper Heart Basket

glue
scissors
2 sheets of paper each 12 x 4 inches (It's best with 2 colors.
    Red and white are good for Valentines.)

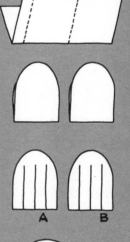

1. Fold each paper in half lengthwise.
2. Round the open edge of the papers.
3. On each paper, make three 4-inch cuts in from the creased edge so you have four strips, each 1 inch wide.
4. Now take one strip from a piece we'll call A and thread it through the first strip of piece B.
5. Now weave by putting the second piece of B through the working piece of A.
6. Thread A *through* the next B piece.
7. Put the last B piece into the A strip.
8. Move A up a little.
9. Now take the second strip of A and thread the first strip of B through it.
10. Continue by going *through* the second strip of B.
11. Put the third strip of B *through* A.
12. And now put A into the last strip of B.
13. Repeat steps 4 through 9 with the third strip of A.
14. Repeat steps 9 through 12 with the last strip of A.
    And there is your *Paper Heart Basket!*

To make a handle, cut another strip of paper the length you want the handle and glue it to each side of the basket.

— Bob Carroll
Glens Falls, New York

CHOPPERS

You will need:

    1 piece of 8½ x 11 inch paper (regular note-
      book size)

    scissors

    pencil, crayons, or paints

Here's what you do:

1. Fold paper in half widthwise.
2. Fold each long edge of paper back to the centerfold.
3. Fold all 4 corners down toward the inside as far as the crease.
4. Hold your paper this way:

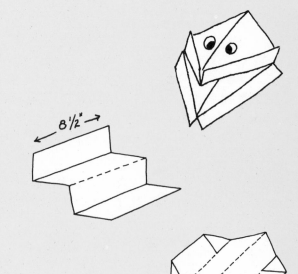

   and fold one top corner to the crease on the front side and the other top corner to the crease on the back.

5. Cut in ½ inch where number 1 is. (Cut through all the folds.)
6. At points 2 and 3, cut off the points — about ½ inch in.

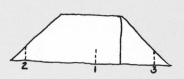

7. Fold the paper up on each side to the top of the ½-inch cut.

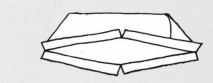

8. Pull out both "1" sides and push 2 and 3 together and there you have it!
9. Funny eyes, nose and other decorations may be added.

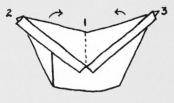

             — Clifford Sjoquist
             South Weymouth, Massachusetts

For a tail for your *Chopper* you will need:
    a piece of 8½ x 11 inch paper (regular note-
      book size)
    scissors
    glue

Here's what you do:

1. Fold the paper in half lengthwise 3 times. When you finish folding, open your paper and it will have 7 long creases.
2. Cut along the creases so you have 8 strips, each of equal width.
3. Glue 4 strips together to form 1 long strip.
4. Glue the other 4 strips together.
5. Now glue the 2 long strips together at a right angle.
6. Fold these strips across each other, on top of the square formed by the glued corner, making neat squares. Alternate one strip with the other until you get to the end of both strips.
7. Glue the ends together and cut off any extra paper. This is the snake's tail.
8. Now glue the tail to the head.

If you want to make a tongue coming out of the *Chopper's* mouth, follow the same steps for making the tail but use skinnier strips of paper. Glue the tongue in the very back of the *Chopper's* mouth.

— Gregory Damarin
Mt. Pulaski, Illinois

Rose and Danny

Streamline Jet Glider

Doug Smythe of Concord, California, makes a *Streamline Jet Glider* that really glides.
I was just experimenting with paper and other things and I accidentally made something. Here are the instructions.

You will need:
    a piece of 8½ x 11 inch paper
    tape

To make the paper jet glider:
1. Fold paper in half lengthwise. Open it out and you have a crease down the middle.

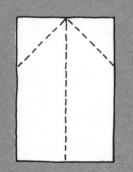

2. Fold the two top corners down to the crease.

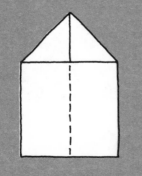

3. Fold side corners in again to the crease.

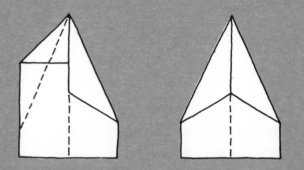

4. Fold two sides together along the original crease.
5. Fold each side back to the center crease line.

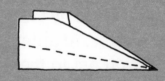

6. Hold the center fold and straighten out the two sides so it looks like a jet glider.

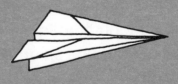

7. Put one small piece of tape on top of the jet in the middle where a triangular point is made by the paper.
8. Test-fly your glider.

Bookcase for Paperbacks

You will need:
  round oatmeal or cornmeal box
  glue
  knife (a serrated one will make it easier)
  self-sticking paper or poster paints
  scissors
  flat piece of wood that is 1 foot long and
    4 inches wide

Here's what you do:
1. Make sure the box is clean. Then glue on the lid tightly.
2. Mark and "saw" out with the knife a section of the box. (Be careful. This is a slow process, and the box may slip out of your hand.)
3. Cover the edges and outside of box with self-sticking paper or paint the box.
4. Glue the back the long way onto the wood so that the box won't roll.

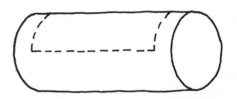

Your books will fit the way shown in the drawing.

— Theresa Warras
Waukesha, Wisconsin

bookcover ZOOMdo

Next time you make your own book cover, use a large old picture calendar for the covering.

— Joan Marler
Salem, Massachusetts

Paper Balloon

1. Take a square piece of paper.
   If your paper isn't square, take any corner and fold it to the opposite side, making a triangle. Cut off the excess paper.

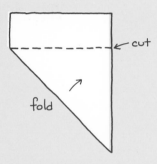

2. Fold your square in half to make a triangle.
3. Open it and fold it again, but use the other 2 corners this time.

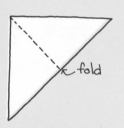

4. Now open the paper and you have a cross in the middle.
5. Bring all 4 sides in together so they meet in the middle.

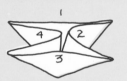

6. Now flatten the paper into 1 triangle.

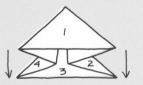

7. Fold each of the 4 corners at the base of the triangle (pyramid) up to the top point of the triangle. (Two corners of one side first, then turn over and do the other.) You have a square.

8. Hold your square so the crease runs up and down.

Fold the 2 outside side corners in so they meet at the crease.

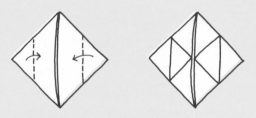

Turn over and do the same on the other side.
9. Each side has 2 loose ends.
   Bring each down across the last fold you made in step 8.

Then fold it back over itself.
Now place it snuggly in the fold below it.
Do all 4.

B-L-O-W!

— Cheryle Pickett
Markham, Illinois

BIG AND BEAUTIFUL BUBBLES

You will need:
tin cans (or paper cups)
scissors (for cutting cups)
tape
shallow bowl
soapy water

1

Remove top and bottom of can so you have a hollow tube. (You can also use paper cups. Cut off the bottom.)

2

Cover rough edges with tape. (Electrical tape would be good for this because it sticks well and is waterproof.)

3

Put one end of can (or paper cup) into soapy water.

4

Blow bubbles through the other end.

Try putting 2 or 3 cans together and see what you get.

— Pam J. Soracco, Peekskill, New York

Egg-Carton Wastebasket

You will need:
- 6 egg cartons (try the Styrofoam kind)
- yarn
- scissors
- paper punch
- pie plate (of aluminum foil)
- plastic bag

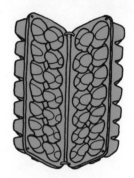

Here's what you do:
1. Cut off the tops of the egg cartons.
2. Punch holes in all four corners of the bottom of each egg carton.
3. Cut twenty-four 2-inch pieces of yarn.
4. Thread yarn through two top holes of two cartons and tie together. Then do the bottom holes.
5. Continue tying all the cartons together.
6. Before tying the last two sections, fit a pie plate into the bottom.
   This may take a little pulling.
7. After tying all the sections together, put a plastic bag as a liner in the basket.

— Sharon Dresser
Chicago, Illinois

Paper Clip Trick

Do you know how to put two paper clips together with a piece of paper?

Here is how you do it:
1. Cut a piece of paper in a long rectangular shape, about 8 inches long and 2½ inches wide.
2. Fold the paper in such a way that the shaded area is between parts A and C as shown.
3. Clip one clip to two layers of the papers, one from A, and one from B. Then clip the other clip to the B and C part.
4. Now hold both ends of the paper with your two hands and pull (gently) at opposite directions.
5. Within one second the two clips are connected.

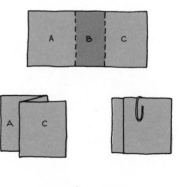

— Elizabeth and Jonathan Peterson
Evanston, Illinois

silhouette pictures

You will need:
- paper
- tape
- a chair
- a lamp
- crayon

To set up for making the pictures:
1. Tape a large sheet of paper to the window.
   A carefully opened bag works well.
   Do not tape it to the wall, as tape leaves marks on the paint.
2. Put a chair and a lamp in front of the paper.
   Leave about a foot or two between the chair and the paper. Put the lamp an inch behind the chair.

What silhouette do you want to make? A plant or toy animal would be good to start on. Here's what you do to make the pictures:
1. Put the toy or plant on the chair.
2. Turn the light on.
3. Take a crayon (black would be best) and trace what you see on the paper.

And there you have it! Do you recognize the picture?
Here is a picture of how to make the silhouettes. After you've practiced doing this a few times, try drawing your friends!

— Elka-Leba Kimmel
Brooklyn, New York

Lisa Louiselle of Horseheads, New York, sent this silhouette.

27

A Boat Story

Dear ZOOM,
Here is an idea that you might like to try. It's a story. But first you must make a boat out of paper.

You will need:
a rectangular piece of paper (regular notebook size will do)

Here's what you do:
1. Fold rectangle in half from top to bottom.

2. Fold 2 corners down from crease to meet each other.

3. Fold up the bottoms, one on each side, so you have a hat.
4. Fold the bottom edges in so you have a triangle.

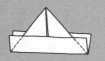

5. Pull out the sides so the bottom points of the triangle come together and you have a square.

6. Fold up the 2 bottom corners, one on each side, to make another triangle.

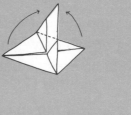

7. With this triangle repeat step 5 so you have another square.
8. With the crease in your square running up and down, grasp the 2 points of the square which open out and pull.

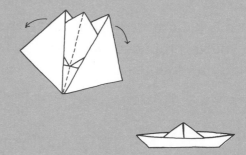

9. Flatten the paper and you have a boat!

Tell the story to someone . . .

Once upon a time, there was a little boat.
It was sailing when it hit an iceberg.
(Bring the boat up to your fist.)

The bow of the boat was torn off.
(Tear off the front.)

The captain backed up, but he hit another
iceberg, and the stern was torn off.
(Tear off the back of the boat.)
A very big storm came and the sail was
torn off by the wind.
(Tear off the center triangle of the boat.)

The little boat sank, and the only thing
that was left was the captain's shirt.
(Open the paper and you'll find the shirt!)

Good luck!

— Lynn Colagiuri (pronounced cola-jury)
Upper Montclair, New Jersey
Catherine and Christine Gervais
Sudbury, Massachusetts

Bird Feeders

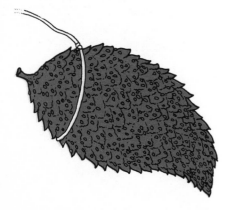

You will need:
  an orange
  knife
  string
  birdseed

Here's what you do:
1. Cut orange in half and clean out the insides so you have just a clean peel.

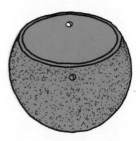

2. Cut two pieces of string and knot one end of each.

3. Put 2 holes (1 on each side) in the peel.
4. Thread the string through the holes.
5. Hang feeder outside.
6. Fill with seed.

It won't last forever, but you can make another one very easily.

— Melissa Maxey
Naperville, Illinois

Or you could:
1. Take a *pine cone.*
2. Spread *peanut butter* all over it and in the cracks.
3. Dip it in a bowl of *birdseed* and roll it all around.
4. Then tie a *string* around it and hang it up in a tree.

The birds love it.

— Jennifer Marrott
Euclid, Ohio

BREAD SCULPTURE

You will need:
    4 cups white flour
    2 cups whole wheat flour
    2 packages of yeast
    2½ cups of warm water
    2 teaspoons of salt
    3 tablespoons sugar, honey, or molasses
    ¼ cup oil
    shortening
    cloth
    tinfoil
    food coloring
    egg yolk

Here's what you do:
1. Measure all the flour into a bowl.
2. In another large bowl, dissolve the yeast in the warm water.
3. Add sugar, salt, and oil to the yeast and water. Mix well.
4. Add the flour.
5. Flour a board or a smooth, clean surface.
6. Knead the dough on the floured surface until smooth.
7. Grease a bowl with shortening.
8. Place the dough in the greased bowl.
9. Cover the bowl with the cloth and let the dough rise in a warm place for an hour.
10. After the dough has risen, take a small piece in your hand and roll it out into any shape you want.
    You can make a sun (happy or sad), a creepy crawly creature, people you know, or even a piece of bread!
11. Put your creation(s) on a piece of tinfoil and bake in a 350 degree oven for 15 minutes or until they are light brown.
12. After the sculpture is baked and cooled, it can be painted with food coloring.
    For a nice finishing glaze, let food coloring dry for at least five minutes, then paint sculpture with egg yolk.

ZOOMdoer: Michelle Ticcolo
Boston, Massachusetts

Clove Air Freshener

You will need:
- an orange
- lots of cloves

1. Push the pointed ends of the cloves into the orange until it's all covered with cloves.
   This takes a while, so you'll have to be patient, but remember that your air freshener will be worth all the effort you've put into it.
2. Tie a ribbon around the middle, leaving enough of the end to hang it up.

> — Anne Beal, Jamaica, New York
> Kevin Cunningham, Brooklyn, New York

Dawn Swanson of Aurora, Illinois, sprinkles cinnamon on top when she is through making one.
David Thayer wrote that he puts his in a nylon net before hanging it in a closet.

Patricia, Mary and Ronnie Bigus of New York, New York, make

Pumpkin Seed Jewelry

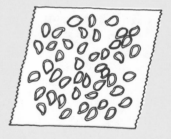

You will need:
- a pumpkin
- cups
- food coloring
- paper towels
- a needle
- heavy black thread

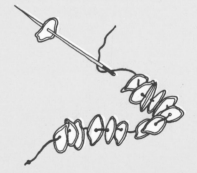

Here's what you do:
1. Just scoop out the seeds from a pumpkin and spread them on paper towels to dry. This may take about an hour.
2. Put the seeds in cups and squeeze some food coloring on them.
3. Stir the seeds with a fork to color them evenly.
4. Spread them on paper towels to dry.
5. When they are dry, string them with your needle and thread.

Stained Glass Cookies

ZOOMdoers Maggie, Peta and Terry Alexander from Newton Centre, Massachusetts, like holding them up to the light and putting their eyes close to them. "We don't really like to eat them, just lick them."

You will need:
    measuring cup
    mixing bowls
    mixing spoon
    sifter
    sour balls
    plastic bags
    hammer
    cookie sheet
    waxed paper

And for the dough:
    ⅓ cup vegetable shortening
    ⅓ cup sugar
    1 egg
    ⅔ cup honey
    3 cups sifted flour
    1 teaspoon baking soda
    1 teaspoon salt

Preheat the oven to 300 degrees at least 15 minutes before you are ready to bake the cookies.

To make the dough:
1. Combine shortening, sugar, egg and honey in a bowl. Mix until everything is one color, and smooth.
2. Sift together the flour, baking soda, and salt into another bowl.
3. Add flour mixture to the honey mixture a little at a time. It's important to keep mixing as you add each ingredient.
4. Now gather the dough you've made in your hands and form it into a ball.
5. Put the dough in the refrigerator to chill, so it won't be so sticky.

To make the colored fillings:
1. Spill out all the sour balls on a table and separate the candy according to color.
2. Put each group of sour balls into separate plastic bags, and use a hammer to crush into pieces. They should not get powdery.
3. Put each color in its own container.

Now make the cookies:
1. Roll out the dough into ¼ inch strips or snakes.

2. Make designs with the dough on a cookie sheet covered with waxed paper.
3. Fill the designs with the crushed candy.
4. Bake in the oven for 8 to 10 minutes.

5. Take the cookies out of the oven. Cut around the waxed paper and put a hole in the candy part if you want to hang them.
6. Let them cool for about 15 minutes.

You can hang them in windows, or do whatever you want with them.

Puppet Cookies

These puppets look and *are* good enough to eat! The batter will make about 6 puppet cookies.

You will need:
    toothpicks
    waxed paper
    gum drops
    pipe cleaners
    basic dough ingredients (below)
    frosting ingredients (below)
    optional:
        cardboard
        string
        a piece of wood

Basic Dough Ingredients:
    ½ cup margerine or butter
    1 cup light brown sugar
    1 egg
    ½ teaspoon vanilla
    2 tablespoons milk
    3 cups flour
    ½ teaspoon salt
    ½ teaspoon baking powder
    ½ teaspoon baking soda

Here's what you do:
1. Cream the butter.
2. Add the sugar. Beat until fluffy.
3. Add egg and vanilla. Mix, add milk.

4. Sift together: flour, salt, baking powder, baking soda.
5. Put these dry ingredients into the mixture and completely blend everything together.
6. Shape the dough into a log and wrap in waxed paper. Put in freezer for ½ hour or in refrigerator for several hours.
7. Then take out enough to make one puppet. (Keep the rest cold.) Place between two pieces of waxed paper and roll to ⅛ inch thickness. Draw design on dough with toothpick and cut.

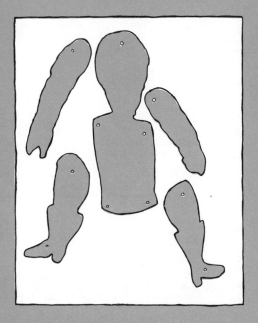

Make sure that the head and body are one unit.
The arms and legs should be separate pieces.

8. Make holes with toothpick so that arms and legs can later be joined to the body.
9. Bake at 400 degrees for 8 to 10 minutes.
10. Let cool thoroughly before you carefully remove with a spatula.

Frosting for decorating:
    3 egg whites
    ⅛ teaspoon cream of tartar
    1 pound confectioner's sugar
    food coloring (to be added later)

Beat all the ingredients (except food coloring) together until the mixture is the consistency of thick paint. Separate into containers and add food coloring to get desired colors.

To assemble puppet cookies:
1. Paint each piece separately and let dry.
2. Cut pipe cleaners in half.
3. Put pipe cleaner through hole of body and each leg and arm.
4. Twist the end in back so that it won't come through.
5. Put a gum drop in front.

Note: the puppets are fairly fragile when they are fresh. If you want to keep them for a long time, you could trace the outside of the baked puppet on cardboard *before assembly.* Attach each piece to the cut-out cardboard with frosting — and then assemble the puppet.

To use as a puppet: you could hold it in your hand and watch the arms and legs move. Or you could tie a string from one of the top pipe cleaners to the other. From the center of that string you could tie a string which would then be attached to a piece of wood.
To use as a marionette: it is necessary to make holes in the hands and feet *before baking.* You could then put strings through those holes and manipulate them from above.

ZOOMdoers: Jenny Lowenthal
David Goldstein
Lea Shapiro
Waban, Massachusetts

Applehead Dolls

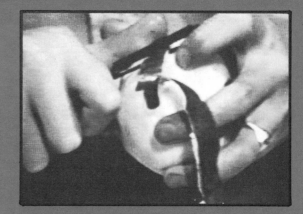

You will need:
    an apple
    a sharp knife (without teeth)
    decoration for the doll (suggestions: costume jewelry, thread, yarn, pieces of material, glue, or needle and thread, buttons, etc.)

Here's what you do:

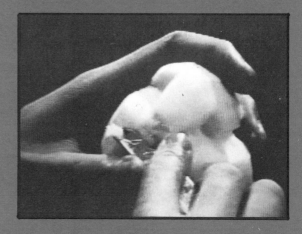

1. Peel the apple, but leave some skin on the bottom.
2. Carve a face into the apple. Make the eyes deeper than the cheeks. The mouth can be a slit or you can paint one on later. (The slit method is best.) It's hard to tell exactly how your apple will dry. (That's part of the fun.)
3. Let the apple dry for at least two weeks. Keep it in a warm, dry place. (You can, of course, work on more than one apple at a time.)
   You'll know that the apple is dry enough when it is very wrinkled and much smaller than it was. Also, the apple won't feel solid inside. During the summer the applehead will probably not get rock-hard, but in the winter it will.

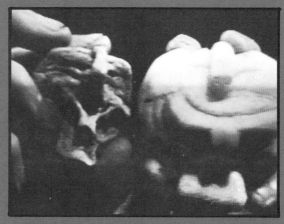

4. When the head is dry make the rest of the doll. The hair can be made out of cotton, fur, or even popcorn. To attach the hair you can either sew it on or use glue. (Be gentle when you sew through the apple. If the stitches are too tight the apple might break. If the stitches are too loose the hair will slide all over the place.)
5. The doll's body can be made any way you like. One way is to sew material together with some stuffing.
   You don't have to make a neck. Sew the material right onto the head.

The doll is now ready to be dressed in any way you choose.

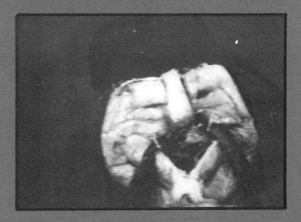

ZOOMdoer: Paul Ginandes
Concord, Massachusetts

HOMEMADE CLAY

Do not eat.

You will need:
    2 cups flour
    ½ cup salt
    ½ cup water
    1 tablespoon cooking oil
    food coloring or paint (optional)

If you want the dough to be colored, put a few drops of food coloring into the water before you pour the water into the mixture.

Here's what you do:
1. Put all ingredients into a bowl and knead for at least 5 minutes.
2. Shape into whatever you want.
3. You can just let it stay the way it is to harden *or* you can put it on a cookie sheet in a 350 degree oven for 1 hour.

When it cools, you can paint it if you want.

— Dena Aldridge
Margate, Florida

Michele Judah of Budd Lake, New Jersey, thinks this recipe is fun and messy.

Doorstop

You will need:
    any old brick
    scraps of material, felt and maybe some yarn
    scissors
    white glue
    enamel house paint

Here's what you do:
1. Wash brick until it is clean.
2. Let it dry overnight.
3. Paint all but the bottom of the brick any color you want or happen to have around the house.
4. Let it dry.
5. Outline brick's bottom on a piece of felt.
6. Glue the rectangle to the bottom of the brick so floors won't get scratched.
7. Now you can decorate the brick with any designs you cut from leftover cloth.

        — Megan Perry
        White Plains, New York

Rock Animals

Here are two ZOOMdos made with rocks.

    rocks
    paper
    paints, crayons
    glue

1. Find big, round rocks.
2. Cut the paper into shapes. If you're going to make a bird you may want to use the shapes shown here.
3. You can color the shapes if you want.
4. Glue them on the rock and there you have it!

You can make any kind of animal.

        — Donna Doyle
        Pargould, Arkansas

Christine Quackenbush of Huntington, West Virginia, calls hers *Rock Critters.*

1. Take some rocks (any size).
2. Glue them together any way you want.
3. Let the glue dry.
4. You don't have to paint them. You can mark them with markers or crayons.

Sand Candles

You will need:
- sand
- shells, beads or stones
- string
- stick
- wood (for a fire on the beach; a stove can be used at home)
- fireplace grill (if you're making the candle on the beach)
- paraffin (wax)
- coffee can
- crayons (old broken ones will do)
- metal pail

Here's what you do:

1. Sprinkle some water on the sand to dampen it. Dig a hole in the sand. Make any size or shape you want.
2. Look for small pieces of wood, stones or shells to decorate the outside of your candle.
3. Place your decorations against the sides of the sand hole. They will show on the outside of your finished candle.

4. Wrap one end of your wick (string) around a stick and place the stick across the hole so that the wick hangs into the hole.
5. If you are making a sand candle on the beach, ask an adult to help you build a fire. Place a fireplace grill over the fire.
6. Now you're ready to melt the paraffin wax. *Read the Caution for Melting Wax*, above.

   You need enough paraffin to fill the hole in the sand.

7. Put the paraffin into the coffee can, add some pieces of crayon for color, and set the coffee can in a pail of water on the stove or on the fireplace grill. Heat until the wax is melted.
8. Slowly pour the melted wax into the sand hole.

   Fill the hole to about an inch from the top.
9. The candle will harden in about 1½ hours.
10. Dig out your candle and cut off the end of the wick.
11. Wash or brush off the extra sand from the candle.

ZOOMdoers: Lisa Gerlinger
San Diego, California
David Dodgen
La Mesa, California

Bayberry Candles

Bayberries grow abundantly on Cape Cod. Andrew and Wendy Titcomb live there in East Sandwich, Massachusetts,

and make *Bayberry Candles* in the fall after they gather berries — before the birds get them. This is how they make candles from the bayberries:

    a bucketful of bayberries will make 2 dipped candles
    a pot
    water
    candle mold, small milk cartons or tin cans
    cheesecloth or gauze
    rubber band
    pencils
    wicks
    2 coffee cans
    salt (to smother any wax fire)

Here's what you do:

1. Put the berries in a pot and pour in water until the berries are completely covered.
2. Bring the water and berries to a boil stirring them sometimes. Keep boiling them until no more wax floats to the surface.
3. Place the cooled pot in the refrigerator until the wax hardens on the surface of the water.
4. Remove the pot from the refrigerator and take out the wax. Break the wax into chunks and put it into a coffee can.
5. Put the coffee can into a pot of water to make a double boiler. Before you begin to heat the wax, read the Caution for Melting Wax on page 39.

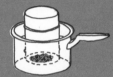

6. Heat the double boiler until the wax melts.

7. Prepare your mold by tying a piece of wick around a pencil. Rest the pencil over the top of the mold. The wick should be long enough to touch the bottom of the mold.
8. Now, take the cheesecloth or gauze and fasten it over the can of melted wax with a rubber band. You're ready to strain the wax.

9. Tip the can and carefully pour the wax into the mold.
10. The wax will harden in about 6 hours. Then remove your candle from the mold. The milk carton will just tear off but a tin can should be dipped into hot water quickly before the candle will slide out.

balancing ZOOMdos

ZOOMers Timmy and Donna

Have someone lie down on the floor. Put a nickel on their nose. They must wrinkle it off their nose. They cannot SHAKE it off. They have to do it by wrinkling their nose and face.

— Kelly Shortt
Camarillo, California

ZOOMer Mike

Place a kernel of popcorn on your shoulder and try to take it off using your tongue.
Try it at home with your friends!

— Heather Carlson
Durham, New Hampshire

ZOOMer Luiz

Try to roll a peanut with your nose. Put a line of tape on the floor. Put another line about 10 feet away and see who can go the farthest.

— Kathleen Impsun

BATIK T-SHIRT

ZOOMdoers: Debbie Green
Paula Gregorio
Mary Earner
South Boston, Massachusetts

You will need:
- pan of water
- muffin tin
- stove (or double hot plate)
- paraffin wax
- wax crayons
- cotton T-shirt (prewashed and dried)
- cardboard box
- paint brushes
- any commercial dye
- iron

Here's what you do:
1. See Caution for Melting Wax on page 39.

   Put the muffin tin over a pan of hot water (not boiling) on the stove.
2. Put a chunk of paraffin and 1 or 2 crayons of a single color in each section of the muffin tin.
3. Stretch the T-shirt over the cardboard box.

   The cardboard will give a smooth surface to paint on.
4. Paint a design on the T-shirt with the melted paraffin-crayon mixture.

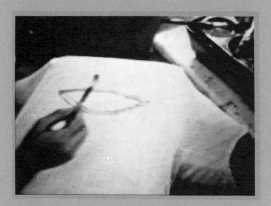

   To prevent colors from getting muddy, use a different paint brush for each color.

   Also, be careful not to get the paint too thick or the wax will flake off.
5. Mix the dye (double strength) with hot tap water.
6. When the mixture is cool, put the T-shirt in to soak for about half an hour — or until the color is darker than you want the shirt to be when it's dry.

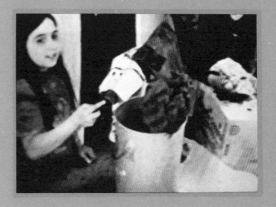

7. Lift the T-shirt out, letting the excess dye drip off.
8. Rinse the shirt in cold water until the water runs clear.
9. Hang it up to dry.
10. Flatten the shirt out on newspaper.
11. Carefully pad the inside of the shirt with layers of newspaper.
12. Put the shirt on a flat surface. Place more layers of newspaper on top of the T-shirt.
13. Press the T-shirt with a hot iron, making sure that you are ironing the paper and not the shirt. (Be sure there's plenty of newspaper to absorb the wax!)

    As you iron, the wax melts into the paper and the color sets into the cloth.

    The longer you iron, the more permanent the color will be.
14. When the T-shirt is dry you can wear it.

    You may want to wash it separately the first few times so any excess dye won't color your other clothes.

Dear ZOOM:

I made this snake: Here's how you can make your own.

You will need:
    bright-colored pieces of felt
    scissors
    white glue

Here's what you do:

1. Cut 1 long strip of felt pointed at one end and shaped like a "Y" on the other end.
2. Cut 8 ovals of felt — each about 1 inch wide. (Trace your first one to make the others exactly the same size.)
3. To make the head, glue 2 ovals together with the long strip between them, letting the "Y" shape stick out for a tongue.
   Glue on 2 small circles for eyes.
4. Glue the other ovals together the same way: 2 at a time with the strip between them to make the body. Leave the pointed end sticking out for a tail.
5. If you want to you can decorate the body ovals with felt flower shapes or dots.

     Love,

     Julie Morse

    Coral Springs, Florida

Snake

yarn dolls

You will need:
  book (about 1½ inches thick)
  yarn
  scissors
  small ball (optional)
  glue
  bits of paper or cloth
  needle
  embroidery thread (optional)

Here's what you do:

1. Wrap yarn around a book until the yarn is quite thick and then slip it off. As you do this, hold onto the ends and make sure the ends are kept even.
2. Tie a piece of scrap yarn at the top, and another where the neck should be.
3. Divide the yarn below the neck into body and arms.
4. Tie the arms where the wrists should be and cut off the extra yarn.
5. Tie at the waist.
6. You can divide the yarn below the waist or leave it like a skirt.
7. You can put a small ball inside the head to make it more solid.
8. To make a face you can glue on pieces of fabric, sew buttons on, or embroider eyes, nose and mouth.

— Pam Robinson

Dirndl Skirt

You will need:
  1½ yards washable fabric
  scissors
  needle and thread
  1 yard of ½ inch wide elastic
  a safety pin

1. Wrap the fabric around you and form a tube loosely around your hips. Then sew a seam down the open side of the skirt.

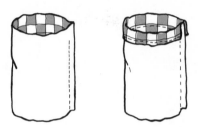

2. Now, fold over the top of the skirt 1 inch and sew a hem for the waistband. Leave a space at the end of the seam for the elastic to poke through.
3. Attach the safety pin to the elastic and bring it through the waistband seam.

Measure elastic by fitting it comfortably around your waist, and then add 1 inch for sewing ends together.

4. Once the elastic is inched through, sew the two ends of the elastic together. Then, sew the waistband opening together.

5. Now, hem your skirt any length you want it.
Wear it!

— Judy Balsamo
Leonia, New Jersey

Bandanna Pillow

Here's an unusual and easy way to make pillows to decorate your room — or just to sleep on.

You will need:
  2 bandannas
  pins
  a needle
  some thread
  stuffing (foam rubber or old pieces of fabric)

Here's what you do:
1. Lay the bandannas flat on a table, one on top of the other with the right sides facing each other.

2. Pin down the edges.
3. Sew around the four edges, *but leave* 6 inches open on one side for stuffing.

4. Turn the pillow covering right side out and fill the pillow with the stuffing.
5. Now, sew the opening up.

There's your pillow!

Sock Puppets

Not long ago I was playing with an old sock, pretending it was a ghost. Then I noticed I was using it like a puppet.

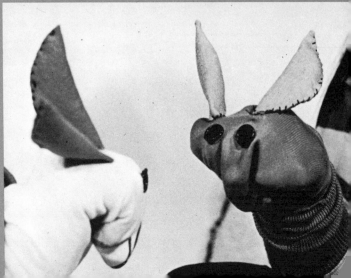

So I got some more *old socks* (a light color) and some *felt-tipped markers* and drew a face.

Then I got some *thread, cotton,* and *another pair of old socks* and cut 4 pieces into the shape of a rabbit's ears.

Then I got a *needle* and using two of the pieces sewed an ear halfway up. Then I used some small pieces of the cotton and stuffed the ear with it. Then I sewed the ear together.

I did the same thing to the other ear. Then I sewed the ears on the puppet.

I had a good time doing this. I hope you will too. (You can make other characters this way — such as a dog, cat, mouse, etc.)

— Karen McCoy
Middletown, Connecticut

DASHIKI

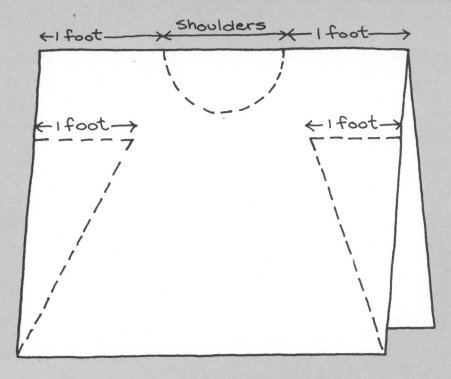

You will need:
  newspaper
  tape measure
  scissors
  2 yards of colorful material
  pins
  needle and thread

Here's what you do:
1. Use the newspaper to make your own pattern.
2. To make the *width* of the pattern: Measure the distance between your shoulders. To that measurement add 24 inches (2 feet) for the arms.

Now you're ready to cut the pattern:
1. Cut a semicircle exactly in the middle for the neck. Be sure it's big enough to get your head through!
2. For the sleeve: From the top edge *measure* down 1 foot, and then from the side *cut* in 1 foot.
3. Do the same for the sleeve on the other side.
4. Cut down from under the arm to the length you want it. Taper it to go out a little bit.

To make the *Dashiki:*
1. Fold the material in half so that the right side is on the inside. Make sure it is as long and as wide as your pattern.
2. Put the pattern on the material so that the neck is on the fold.
3. Pin the pattern to the material.
4. Cut around the pattern.
5. Sew up both sides about 1 inch from the edge. Be sure not to sew up the arm holes or the bottom!
6. Turn the material right side out.
7. Hem the neckline, sleeve edges, and the bottom.

blue jeans bag

If you use an old pair of jeans to make a book bag or pocketbook, you can put things like a comb in one of the pockets.

You will need:
    an old pair of jeans or pants
    scissors
    needle
    thread
    snaps or hooks

Here's what you do:

1. Cut your pants about here:

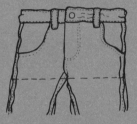

2. Turn pants inside out.
3. Sew the front and back of the blue jeans together along the new bottom that you have just cut.
4. Open the seam that you have just sewn and iron it flat.
5. Turn the blue jeans right side out.
6. To make a strap, cut a strip of material from the blue jeans leg or some other material that is long enough for you. Make the strip about 6 inches wide.

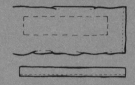

7. Turn this strip wrong side out and sew it together lengthwise about ½ inch from edge.
   When you are finished turn it inside out so the good side is on the outside.

8. Sew strap to the sides of the bag.
9. If you want it to stay closed, sew snaps along the top.

— Erika Hansen
Seattle, Washington

hula skirt

I live in Hawaii. I am going to show how to make ti (tē) leaf hula skirt. Any big leaf will do.

You will need:
    20 to 30 ti leaves, or any big leaves
    a piece of string long enough to go around your waist 1½ times

Here's what you do:

1. String the leaves on the string (at one end of the leaf) overlapping leaves. Allow enough string at each end for tying around your waist.
2. Put the hula skirt around your waist and tie in the back.

— Carrie Klett
Eewa Beach, Hawaii

TIE-DYEING

You will need:

    dye (3 different colors give you a good variety and powdered dye is easy to work with.)

    1 cup

    salt

    water

    cloth (cotton which has been washed 2 or 3 times — like an old sheet. Don't use perma press or synthetics.)

    scissors

    string or rubber bands

    old pans (1 for each color dye. Certain dyes stain the pans so be sure to read instructions on dye package.)

    Note that dye can be washed off a *glass* cup and *enamel* pans.

    hot plate or stove

To mix the dye, follow the instructions on the dye package. If you want your dye to be darker, just add more equal amounts of salt and dye. *Keep the dye hot* (but not boiling) on the stove or hot plate.

Before you start Tie-Dyeing, try out the dye on samples of cloth to see if the colors are as bright as you'd like them to be.

For a sunburst effect:

1. Wet a white piece of cloth.
2. Hold it at the center and bring all the corners down together.
3. Now tie 3 or 4 strings or rubber bands (about an inch apart) around the cloth as in the drawing.

4. Dip the cloth in the lightest dye for 1 or 2 minutes. (Save the darkest dye for last.)
5. Take it out of the dye and rinse it in cold water.
6. To add the next color, take off one or two strings *where you want the next color to be.* Put more strings *wherever you want the cloth to stay the last color you used.*
7. Then dip again in the same way, including rinsing with cold water.
8. Finish by repeating the process with the darkest color dye.
9. Rinse with cold water until the water runs clear.
10. Open up your cloth and you've got a sunburst.

Helpful hints:

1. Tie all strings and knots very tight.
2. Remember to wash anything you've dyed separately in cold water — or it can be dry cleaned.

One of the hardest things is taking off the strings.

    ZOOMdoer: Tim Mapel
    Lexington, Massachusetts

Make Your Own Music

Water
Glass jars
Spoon

1. Put water in glass jars or juice glass or soda bottles. Put 2 inches in one, 3 inches in another, about 4 inches in another and maybe 6 inches of water in another.
2. Take a spoon and tap the glass.
3. See what kind of music you can come up with.

— Brenda Campbell
Bronx, New York

Beach Glass

I collect glass. This isn't ordinary glass. It's beach glass. Beach glass isn't like any other glass. It's all smooth and there are no sharp points.
The best time to get beach glass is when it's low tide at the beach. What you do is go down by the water and find it down there.

When you get home you wash the sand off the glass and put it in a clear jar of water. Then put it where light can get at it. It will be beautiful.

— Susan McGuiness
Levittown, New York

Ocean In A Bottle

You will need:
   a bottle (preferably one with squared sides so it can lie on its side)
   blue or green food coloring
   cooking oil
   white vinegar

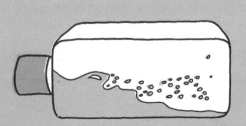

Here's what you do:
1. Fill about ⅓ of the bottle with white vinegar.
2. Add blue or green food coloring to color the vinegar.
3. Fill the rest of bottle to the top with cooking oil.
4. Secure the top and then rock your "wave maker" gently back and forth.

There's a lot to watch!

— Diane White
Hanover, Massachusetts

String Sculpture

You will need:
    a balloon
    string or yarn
    white glue (or liquid starch)

Here's what you do:
1. Blow up the balloon and knot it.
2. Dip string or yarn in the glue (or starch). A good coat of glue is necessary. (If you're using yarn, run the yarn lightly through your fingers to get excess liquid out.)
3. Wrap the string or yarn around the balloon.
4. Let it dry. (You could put it in a bowl or just hang it someplace.) It may take a few days before it is completely dry.
5. Pop the balloon and gently take out all the pieces through the string sculpture.
6. To hang, tie a string around the top.

> — Brenda Olney
>   Richardson, Texas
>   Elizabeth Savramis
>   Portsmouth, New Hampshire
>   Elisabeth Wibbelman
>   Mount La Keterr, Washington

STRING ART

You could use nails on a board for this.

    paper (construction paper is best)
    pencil
    needle
    tape
    thread

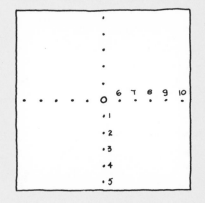

Here's what you do:

1. Make a pattern and number your points on the back of the paper.
2. Now thread your needle and bring it up through point 5 and down through 6.
3. Go up through the paper at point 7 and down through point 4. Go up at point 3 and down at point 8 and so on.
4. Do the center point last.

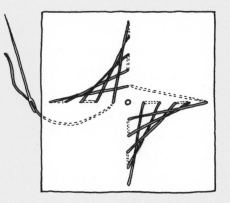

You can increase the number of points on each spoke to make a larger design. And, you can increase the number of spokes to make your design more complex.

— Chuck Lingler
Mt. Prospect, Illinois

Button and String Game

My mother is French and she told me that this game is called "frawn" in French.

You will need:
    a long piece of string
    a big button that has at least 2 holes

Here's what you do:
1. Cut the string to measure 30 inches.
2. Thread the string through one hole, then the next.
3. Tie the ends of the string together.
4. Put your fingers through the ends.
5. Then you wind it up with a circling motion. (Try winding it toward you as if you were swinging a jump-rope.)
6. When it's all wound up (about 25 times), pull your hands away from each other and then in and out with the rhythm of the string. The button will go around and around.

                  — Don Bernard
                   Gretna, Louisiana

All these flower ZOOMdos were sent in by Sabra Temsky of Worcester, Massachusetts.

Dried Flowers

To preserve fresh flowers you will need:
    cornmeal
    borax
    a box that is about 6 inches deep
    a dry paint brush (optional)

Here's what you do:
1. Mix equal parts cornmeal and borax.
2. Pour this mixture into the box until it's about 1 inch deep.
3. Carefully lay the flowers onto the mixture, upside down.
4. Gently sift on more mixture, trying not to crush petals while getting the mixture in between the petals.
5. Leave buried for two weeks.
6. Gently remove from mixture.
7. If necessary, clean petals with a dry paint brush.

Use in covered jars for decoration, on birthday cakes or on gift packages.

Pressed Flowers

You can use all sorts of flowers:
    wild flowers
    garden flowers
    blooms from house plants

Try to find flowers that are going to press flat (without bumpy middles). Pick them after the morning dew has dried.

Here's what you do:
1. Press the flowers between *2 pieces of tissue paper* in a *thick book.* Do not crowd the blooms.
2. Place more books or other heavy objects on top of the book containing the flowers.
3. Wait two weeks before you use them.

pressed flower note paper

1. Fold plain *white paper* in half to form note card. (You'll use this as a pattern for the next step.)
2. Open flat under a piece of *waxed paper* cut the same size.
3. Arrange flowers on waxed paper.
4. Cover with a sheet of *rice paper* (cut the same size as the note and waxed paper).
5. Paint rice paper with a mixture of half *white glue* and half *water*.
6. When the glue is dry, remove note card.
7. Lay the rice paper-waxed paper sandwich on a *dish towel* on an *ironing board*.
8. Put a sheet of waxed paper (any size) over it.
9. Put a piece of *heavy brown paper* (cut one from a grocery bag) over this.
10. Press with a warm *iron*. (The heat will force the glue through the rice paper and make a sealed sandwich.)
11. Peel off the top waxed paper layer. (The top waxed paper sheet may be used 4 times, twice on each side.)
12. Fold rice paper sandwich in half.
13. Place note card inside pressed flower cover.
14. Write to a friend!

pressed flower picture

You will need:
    fabric (A scrap piece is good. Flowers will stick on velvet or corduroy.)
    a picture frame with glass (Maybe there's an old one not being used that would be fine.)
    glue is optional (You can use it to make the flowers stick to the fabric.)

Here's what you do:
1. Cut the fabric a little larger than the frame you are using.
2. Put the pressed flowers on the fabric. You may want to use a little glue to make them stick.
3. Lay on the glass, trying to keep the flowers from moving.
4. Slip fabric into the frame.

MAZE

You will need:
  1 pencil with eraser
  clock, watch *or* timer

Instructions:
Starting from either point A, B, C, or D, find the path to the *end*.
Time limit: *3 minutes.*

— Robert O'Koniewski
Albany, New York

Glue Dos

All you need is some *white* glue and a *piece of waxed paper.*
Take the glue and write a word. Connect all the letters as you are writing.
Then let it dry until it is *all* clear. (Sometimes it takes at least a day to dry.)
Then slowly peel it off and color it with felt-tipped pens.

— Sue Kostelny and Pam David
Chicago, Illinois

Donna Merenda of New Alexandria, Pennsylvania, does it a little differently.
First you put *glue* in a *jar lid* (use one that doesn't have grooves or a cardboard seal) and wait at least three or four days for it to dry clear. Then take it
out and paint it any way you want.

Découpage

To decorate glass jars or bottles you will need:
    glue
    water
    tissue paper (colored)
    a small paint brush

Here's what you do:
1. Mix glue with water to make a soupy mixture.
2. Tear tissue paper into pieces.
3. Dip pieces into glue and water mixture.
4. Put them on the jar and keep overlapping the paper.
5. After you're finished and it's dry, put one more coat of glue and water over the whole thing.

    — Donna Salter and Diane Seltzer
    East Brunswick, New Jersey

    Melinda Minzey
    Elkhart, Indiana

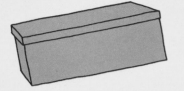

You can also use découpage to make a storage box.

You will need:
   magazines
   scissors
   a shoe box
   glue
   shellac
   a paint brush

1. Cut out different pictures from magazines. (You could use a theme such as food or toys.)
2. Glue them all over the box without leaving any spaces.
3. Then paint the whole box with shellac.

You could put découpage on a can or anything you can think of.

— Alexis Rabasca
College Point, New York

Try découpage to make a hanging. You will need:
   a piece of thin wood
   wood stain
   picture from magazine or card
   glue
   clear varnish
   paint brush
   thumbtacks, hanging wire (optional)

Here's what you do:
1. Stain the wood and let it dry for an hour.
2. Cut out picture you want to use and make sure it's smaller than your piece of wood by at least ½ inch on all sides.
3. Glue picture to wood after stain is dry.
4. Put a coat of clear varnish over the picture and let it dry.
5. To hang, put thumbtacks into back of wood and attach wire.

— Lisa and Michael Quadrino
Sheri Denker
Baldwin, New York

Dear Zoom,
Here is a way of making chin puppets,
to do it you need: lipstick
                        eyebrow pencil
                        hankercheif
                        Mirror
First of all to do it is like making an
upside down face on your chin.
   Use eyebrow pencil for nose, eye and lipstick for
the mouth.

Then flip your head over the
end of a table or chair like
so.

Then blindfold yourself like it looks in
the picture.

                        your done!
                    Move your lips to make it
                    work.

   You can make the puppet more interesting by
drawing on a mustache, eyelashes, etc.

                        FROM,

                        JANICE OKANISHI
                        ROSEMEAD, CALIFORNIA

Block Prints

Here's how to make meat package prints. It's very easy once you know how. I used mine to make this stationery.

— Bo Newsome
Harrisburg, Pennsylvania

You will need:
    Styrofoam meat package
    dull pencil
    sheets of newspaper
    tube of block printing ink (any color)
    sheet of glass
    block printing roller
    sheets of white paper

Here's what you do:
1. Engrave a picture into the Styrofoam package with the dull pencil.
2. Spread some newspaper wherever you are working.
3. Squeeze some block printing ink onto the sheet of glass and roll the roller back and forth in the ink until the roller is covered with the ink.
4. Now, roll the roller over the engraved side of the Styrofoam package.
5. Take the inked package and press it against a piece of white paper. Remove, and now you have a print.

You can use the Styrofoam engraving over again.

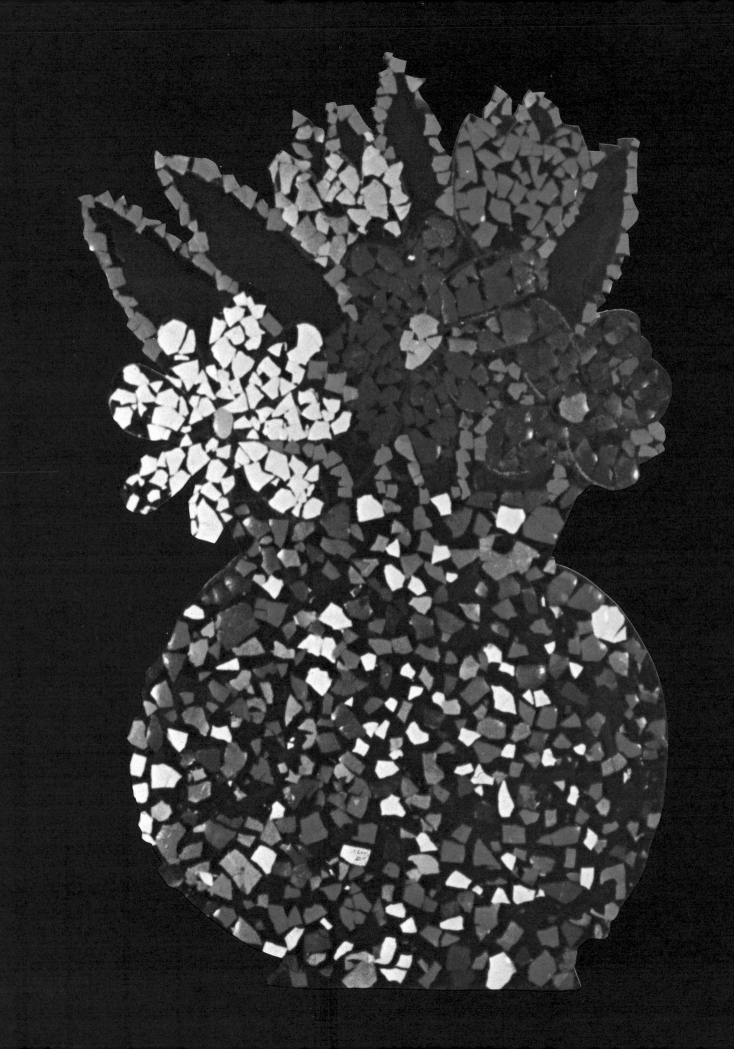

Eggshell Art

You will need:
    heavy paper (construction paper is fine)
    eggshells (a whole bunch)
    food coloring
    water
    glue
    paper

Here's what you do:
1. Crush the eggshells. (You may want to have some large pieces and some very small.)
2. Mix the eggshells and separate them into a few groups.
3. Color the eggshells. A good way to dye with food coloring is to put eggshells in a jar, add a few drops of food coloring and water. Put the cover on the jar and shake until the eggshells are colored. Then spread the eggshells on a newspaper to dry.
4. With glue make a design on a piece of heavy paper.
5. Sprinkle the glue design with the different-colored eggshells.
6. Just let dry.

— Deanna Newman, El Dorado, Kansas
Ruth and Cenci DeRomero, Bronx, New York

Other ideas:
Sonnette Lowe of Chicago, Illinois, covers her design with waxed paper and then puts about 4 books on the picture until it dries.
"It takes about 5 minutes. It depends on how many books you use."
Jessica Horton of Ardmore, Tennessee, gets her color a different way. She sprinkles on plain crushed eggshells and lets her picture dry in the sun. And then she paints the picture.

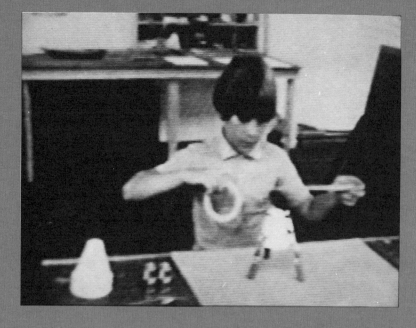

DRAWING

You will need:
    3 felt markers (use any colors you want)
    masking tape
    a plastic cup
    2 size-D batteries
    lightweight electrical wire
    a paper clip
    a 1½ volt electrical motor
    a metal nut, washers, or a small heavy object
    lots of drawing paper

Here's what you do:
1. Tape the 3 markers around the cup so that it makes a tripod.
   The tips should point down, and should extend 2 inches lower than the rim of the upside-down cup.
2. Tape a battery on the side of the cup next to one of the pens with the + side level with the rim of the cup.
3. On the other side of the cup tape the other battery with its — side level with the cup's rim.
4. Cut a piece of wire the length of the distance between the batteries under the rim of the cup.
5. Strip both ends of the wire.
6. Tape one end to the — side of one battery and the

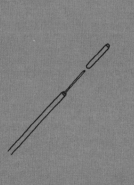

MACHINE

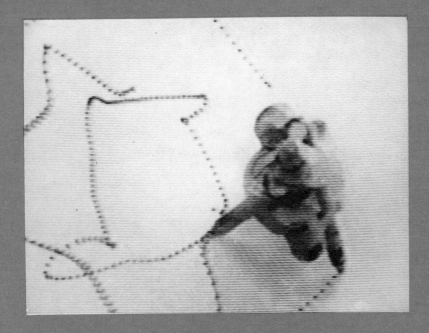

other to the + side of the other battery.

7. Take a paper clip and straighten it.
8. Tape one end of the paper clip to the rotating axle of the motor.
9. Attach the other end to the nut or washers.
   Make sure the tape is very secure. This is the weight which helps balance the machine.
10. Tape the motor to the top of the plastic cup, with axle and weight pointing up. Use lots of tape as it has to be secure.
11. Tape one of the two wires from the motor to the top of one battery.
12. Now the other wire should be taped to the top of the other battery. As soon as the second wire is attached the motor will start, and the weight will begin to spin around.
13. Take the caps off the pens, and let the machine go on the paper. It will take off on its own, and draw a picture for you!

Hints: You can change the general pattern of the picture by bending the paper clip so that the weight is nearer or farther from the machine.
If you have an old picture frame, put it on your piece of paper. This will keep the machine from wandering.

ZOOMdoer: Tim Mamis
Brookline, Massachusetts

Homemade Paint

How would you like to make your own paints? It's simple. Here's how you do it.

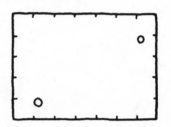

You will need:
  a small jar
  ½ teaspoon of vinegar
  ½ teaspoon of cornstarch
  about 10 drops of food coloring

Here's what you do:
1. Put vinegar and cornstarch in the jar.

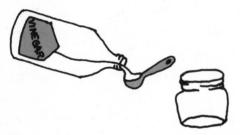

2. Put 10 drops of food coloring in the jar.

3. Shake it all up and there's your paint! If the paint is too thin, add more cornstarch. If it's too thick, add more vinegar.

— Yvonne Legan
Clark, New Jersey

Ruler Designs

Lisa Kalaha of Dickson City, Pennsylvania, likes to make *Designs with a Ruler*. Here's how:

1. On a sheet of paper make 2 large dots placed diagonally.

2. Then all around the sheet draw small dots about 2 inches apart.
3. After that, draw a line from each small dot to one of the large dots.

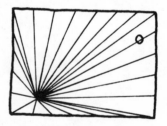

4. Draw a line from each small dot to the other large dot.
5. It should turn out like this:

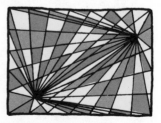

6. Color the blocks of the design. You can either make them different colors or use only two.

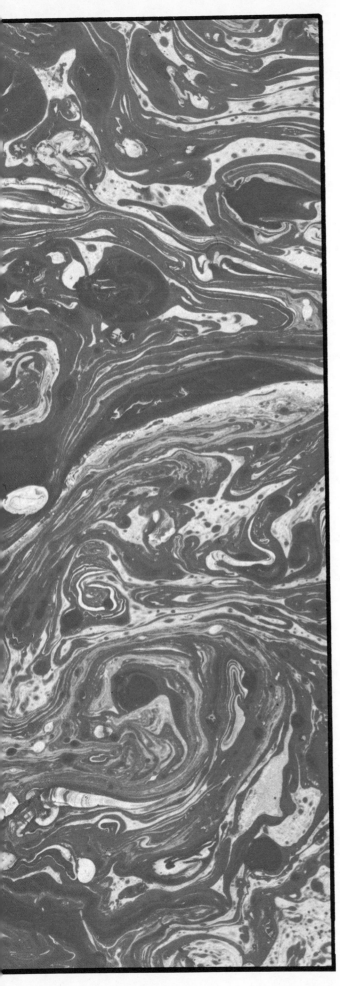

Marbleized Paper

You will need:

a rectangular container. Try to find one that you can mess up. An aluminum broiling pan may do.

turpentine

oil based paint. Use tubes available from an art supply store. If you use house paint, be careful to work slowly so that it doesn't have to be thinned too much. You can use one or several colors to make your design.

some small jars or paper cups

paintbrush

white paper

Here's what you do:

1. Fill pan with an inch or two of water.
2. Pour a little turpentine in a jar.
3. To the turpentine add some oil paint, a little at a time until the color is rich and the mixture is the consistency of milk.
4. Mix up other colors in the rest of the jars.
5. Dip a paintbrush in one color. *Drip* it onto the surface of the water in the pan. Be careful not to dip the brush in the water.

   Do the same with the other colors. (If you're using more than one color.)
6. To get the marbleized effect, you now swirl the paint (gently) with a stick.
7. Briefly lay a piece of white paper on the surface of the water.
8. Let the paper dry.
9. When they're dry, you can mount the pictures on cardboard or frame them.

The best part is that each design is totally unique.

— Fred Albert
Waban, Massachusetts

SELF PORTRAIT

Blindfold yourself and try to draw your own self portrait.
Good luck!

— Laurie Schmitz, Clayton, Missouri

Randi Meberg
Old Toppa, New Jersey

Kim Erlandson
Westford, Massachusetts

Phaedra Oubre
Edgar, Louisiana

Michelle Hill
Rockford, Illinois

Lori Meberg
Old Toppa, New Jersey

Stacey Kerwin
Rochester, New York

exept for this square of writing, I did'nt PEEK" once Love Romessa

Romessa Khan
Ontario, Canada

71

breathless art

How would you like to make a painting without using a brush?
Instead of a brush, you'll use a drinking straw and lots of lung power.

You will need:
    a piece of construction paper
    some old newspaper
    liquid food coloring, poster paint, or ink
    a drinking straw

Here's what you do:
1. Place newspapers under your art paper so that your working place will be neat.
2. Put a drop of color on your piece of paper.
3. Put your straw next to the drop of color and blow hard. Keep blowing to make a color streak.
4. After blowing streaks in one direction, turn the paper to blow in a different direction.
5. Add drops of other colors and follow the same procedure.
6. When you run out of breath, stop and let your paint dry.

— Maria Civitareale
Malden, Massachusetts

sand painting

You will need:
    food coloring
    sand
    a piece of cardboard or heavy construction paper
    glue

Here's what you do:
1. Use food coloring to dye the sand different colors.
2. Draw a picture onto your paper or cardboard.
3. Put glue on one area of the picture and put sand of one color on the area.
4. Let it dry.
5. Shake the paper gently so that the excess sand comes off.
6. Put glue on another area and follow the same procedure.
7. Do this until your design is done.

It's easy and fun.

— Heavenly Reels
Providence, Rhode Island
Pamela Suttenberg
Syosset, New York

Food Coloring Art

Dear ZOOM:

This is made with:
   one paper towel
   four food coloring colors

1. Fold the paper towel until you have a square.
2. Make a design by dripping the colors on the towel.

Don't mix the colors or you'll get an ugly black. It is all right if some of the colors run together. Have fun!

Your friend,
Carl Nooner
Corpus Christi, Texas

P.S. If you don't have food coloring, use different colors of a thick paint.

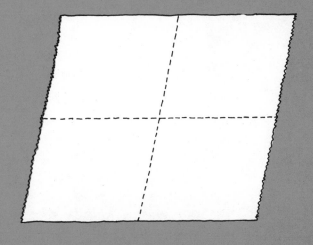

Silk Screening

Make your own silk screen pictures and posters at home!

You will need:
 cardboard
 scissors
 masking tape
 plain organdy
 wheat paste (wallpaper paste)
 a mixing bowl for the paste
 poster paint
 containers and spoons for the paint
 stencil paper (newsprint, tracing paper)
 printing paper (any medium or heavy weight paper will do)

Here's what you do:
1. Cut a frame out of cardboard.

2. Then cut another piece of cardboard the same size and shape as the frame, but without a hole in the middle.
3. Tape the two pieces together with masking tape. They should open like a book.

4. Cut a piece of organdy a little larger than the opening in the frame, and attach it to the inside of the frame with masking tape. You now have your screen.

5. With a small piece of cardboard make a squeegee (a rectangle about ½ inch smaller than the opening of the frame).
6. Mix the wheat paste according to the directions on the package. It should look like a pudding or applesauce.
7. Add a few tablespoons of poster paint.
8. Cut out a stencil, using newsprint

or tracing paper. You can cut any shape you want, but be sure to stay within the size of the cutout frame.

9. Open the screen and place a piece of printing paper on the solid piece of cardboard.

10. Put your stencil on top of the printing paper.

11. Close the screen, and put a lot of paint along the top edge of the screen.

12. Push the paint to the bottom of the screen with the squeegee. You might have to work the paint down to the bottom several times.

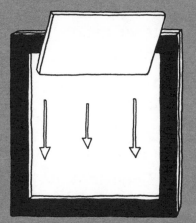

13. Open the screen. The stencil should be stuck to the screen, and the print will be on the printing paper. If the paint is too light on the pictures, you can add more color.

14. Put another piece of paper inside, and print again.

Helpful Hints:
You can use the same stencil over and over again.
If you want to change designs, peel the stencil off the frame, and cut a new one.
To print in another color, wash the organdy screen, or change screens.
You can print more than one color and design on a print, but be sure to let the first color dry before you do.

ZOOMdoers: Rose Ann Salvucci
Caroline Killilea
Geraldine Killilea
Brighton, Massachusetts

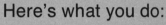

thumbprint art

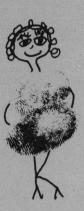

You will need:
ink pad
paper
crayons or felt-tipped pens

Here's what you do:
1. Ink up your fingers — tips, pads and sides.
2. Press them onto paper.
3. With crayons or pens, add your own lines to complete the print.

— Linda Nielsen, Wallingford, Pennsylvania
Jennifer Stewart, Newington, Connecticut
Susan Elmer, Convent Station, New Jersey
Phyllis Labanowski, Troy, New York

Susan writes that the best way to remove ink pad ink from fingers is to use soap and water as soon after finger-printing as possible. Sometimes this must be repeated five or six times. Although your fingers may not come completely clean, this will keep you from leaving finger-prints all over your house!

I am deaf. I communicate with sign language and voice. This is

The Manual Alphabet

-as it looks to the person <u>reading</u> it.   -as it looks to the person <u>spelling</u> it.

Papier-Mâché Piñata

Jose and Miriam Ruiz of Boston, Massachusetts, made a piñata with their friends and hung it from a tree when they had a party.

To make a piñata, you will need:
    lots of old newspaper
    a shopping bag
    string
    large mixing bowl
    ½ pound of wheat paste (This is the
        kind used in hanging wallpaper.)
    egg cartons and cardboard
    masking tape
    paint and brushes
    plastic baseball bat (or long card-
        board cylinder)

Here's what you do:
 1. Tear off lots of strips of newspaper that are about 2 x 8 inches.
 2. Stuff a shopping bag completely with wadded-up newspapers and tie up the end of the bag with some string.

 3. Slowly pour about ½ pound of wheat paste into 8 cups of water in a bowl. Keep stirring till it's nice and gooey.

 4. Soak the paper strips in the paste and cover the bag *completely* with them. (You may wish to add more than one layer of newspaper.)

 5. Allow the bag to dry. (It may be necessary to let it sit overnight.)
 6. Give the bag more personality by adding a nose and eyes. The round sections of an egg carton make good eyes and you can use a small cardboard cylinder for the nose.
    Attach the eyes and nose with masking tape.
 7. After attaching nose and eyes, cover the entire bag with another layer of newspaper strips which have been soaked in paste.
 8. Let the bag dry.
 9. Paint it any way you like.
10. When the paint dries, cut a neat, round opening in the top of the bag and keep the resulting disc so it can be put back.

11. Remove all the crumbled newspaper from the inside and fill it with wrapped candy, little toys or other things you choose.
12. Glue or tape the top back on.
13. Get together with some of your friends and hang the piñata high enough so that somebody swinging the plastic bat or cardboard cylinder can just reach it.
14. Then take turns trying to break the piñata so that all the goodies come out. Each person should be blindfolded and turned around three times before he takes his turn. It's up to you to decide how long the turn should be — or how many tries each person gets.
15. Stay out of the way of the bat!

puppets

You will need:
> newspaper
> toilet paper roll
> flour and water *or* wheat paste
> poster paints
> yarn
> glue
> shellac
> scissors
> cloth

Here's what you do:

1. Crumble newspaper into a ball leaving a "tail" on it.
2. Insert tail into toilet paper roll. This forms head and neck.
3. Mix wheat paste *or* flour and water until it gets gummy.
4. Tear off strips of newspaper.
5. Dip them in the paste one at a time and cover the head and neck, leaving the hole at the bottom end of the neck open.
6. The nose and eyes can be made by putting an extra amount of pasty newspaper where these features should be.
7. Cover the puppet and its features with a few more layers of papier-mâché.
8. Let dry.
9. Paint the head any colors you want.
   Let dry.
10. Glue yarn to the head to make hair.
11. Shellac and let dry.
12. Put points of scissors up in the neck and snip away excess paper so your fingers fit in the neck.
13. You may want to make a body out of cloth and glue it to the neck.

ZOOMdoers: Theresa Willingham
Kiki Konidis
Victor Velazquiz
Billy Dardonis
David Wong
Jean Tse
Boston, Massachusetts

Mâché dos

bowl

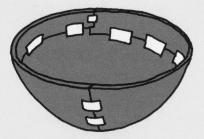

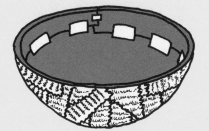

You could make a *Bowl* instead of a puppet — by using a bowl upside down.

1. Cover the outside of the *bowl* with a big piece of *waxed paper*.
   Tape the waxed paper to the inside of the bowl to hold it in place.
2. Spread a thin layer of *soaked-with-mixture news-paper* over the bowl and press down firmly and smoothly around the bowl.
3. Let it dry for a day or two.
4. Remove the bowl you used as the mold.
5. Paint.
6. You may wish to shellac the bowl to make it glossy and help it to keep for a long time.

— Laurie Cantalupo
Bridgeport, Connecticut

beads

You could make *Beads* with the dipped newspaper strips.
Wrap the *strips* around a *knitting needle* — in little clumps.
Let them dry. Remove from needle.
Paint.
String.

Chicken Wire Sculpture

This is a great group ZOOMdo.

Geronimo Jackson is made by Penny Shibley, Darryl Drumgold and Shawn Drumgold.

You will need:
  a saw
  two 6-foot lengths of 2 x 4 inch wood
    (*Note:* used wood will do)
  one 14-inch square piece of ¾ inch ply-
    wood (two scrap pieces could be
    made into a 14 inch square)
  one 1 x 2 inch piece of wood
  16 feet of 3-foot width chicken wire (it's
    3 feet top to bottom when it's in a roll)
  heavy gloves
  wire clippers
  staple gun (U-shaped staples and a
    hammer could be used instead)
  papier-mâché (see page 80)
  water-base paint
  fabric (scraps would be all right)
  yarn (thick) and other scraps for
    trimming
  a cloth mop
  some cork scraps
  cardboard tubes
  two balloons

To make the base:
1. One of the 6-foot pieces should be cut so that you have one 16-inch piece and two 15-inch pieces.
2. Place the 15-inch pieces perpendicular to the 16-inch piece and form the very bottom by nailing these pieces onto a 14-inch square piece of plywood.

3. Now take the other 6-foot length of 2 x 4 and saw with the grain down the middle. The result is a 2-inch square by 6-foot piece to be used as a post to hold up the sculpture.
4. The post should be mounted into the middle of the 14-inch square. Nail it until it is secure.

To make the braces:
1. Use the 1 x 2 inch wood and cut it into four 7-inch pieces. Cut each piece on each end at a 45 degree angle.

2. Nail each piece against the pole.

To prepare the body:
1. Cut the chicken wire with gloves on your

hands. Each piece has a specific measurement.
  — for each arm cut a piece 15 inches wide
  — for each leg you need a piece 17 inches wide
  — the body is made from a piece that is 56 inches
  — the head is made from a 33-inch piece

2. Each cut piece of chicken wire is then hand shaped into a cylinder.

3. Once shaped, fold rough cut edges into each other to hold the shape of the cylinder together.
   Do this for each piece of the body.
4. The head piece should be squeezed together at the bottom half of the cylinder to form the neck.
5. Close off the top of the head by forcing the sides of the cylinder inward.

To mount the body:
1. Put the head onto the stand by slipping it onto the top of the base. With a staple gun, fasten it to the base. (Or use a hammer and staples.)
2. Now other pieces of the body are attached by opening the sealed ends of the chicken wire cylinders with wire clippers. Then you fold the resulting jagged ends into the already mounted part of the chicken wire body. (Be sure to wear gloves during this procedure.)

3. Cover the entire body with papier-mâché. (See page 80 for instructions on making papier-mâché.) One layer is enough, but be sure to overlap each strip with another as you go along.
4. Allow to dry overnight.

Paint your sculpture with water-base paint.

To dress the sculpture:
1. Make the clothing by holding the fabric up to the model and drawing an outline of the clothing you want with crayon or a piece of chalk. Then cut the fabric. It is not necessary to hem anything.
2. Glue the clothing to the painted sculpture. Trim with yarn (the thick kind is best) or other scraps of material.
3. For hair you can use a cloth mop which can be painted (before you put it on the sculpture) with water-base paint.
4. Choose other scraps (maybe some cork) for facial features.

For Geronimo Jackson's barbell the ZOOMdoers taped together cardboard tubing and then tied balloons onto the end of the cardboard. The balloons are covered with one layer of papier-mâché.

Here's another chicken wire sculpture made at the Children's Art Center in

Boston. It is covered with tissue paper (découpage) instead of being painted.

Try your own sculpture!

ZOOMphenomenon

Put two teaspoons of baking soda into an empty balloon. Then put one inch of vinegar into an empty soda pop bottle. Fit the neck of the balloon onto the bottle. Watch closely.

— Censeor Gailey
Chicago, Illinois

Cornstarch Phenomenon

Karen Robinson of Somerville, Massachusetts, thinks you'll find that this is an unusual, fun DO:

You will need:
    a bowl
    cornstarch
    water

Here's what you do:
1. In a bowl, mix about ½ box of cornstarch with enough water so that it feels like clay — not too powdery, not too wet.
2. Knock on the mixture (inside the bowl) and you will find that it feels hard.
3. Put your finger slowly into it and . . . it is liquid!
4. Mold a handful into a ball.

As soon as you stop molding it, it melts in your hand. It's solid one minute, liquid the next.

Ice Cube Phenomenon

Try and pick up
an ice cube with a piece
of string while the ice cube
is floating on the water.

— Paul Vázquez
Jersey City, New Jersey

Answer on page 112.

hand - ear - elbow

Put your right hand on your right ear. Put your left hand on your nose. Try sliding your right elbow through your left arm. Then slide your right hand through without taking your fingers off your nose.

— Nancy Brennan
Fairport, New York

Cornrowing

Cornrowing, a hairstyle, got its name because the parts in the hair look like rows of corn. In Africa, cornrowing has been done for many thousands of years. In America only small children used to wear cornrowing. It helped their hair grow and kept it neat. But today, people of all ages wear cornrowing.

Cornrowing can be done simply — or elaborately. The hairstyle can be decorated by putting colorful beads in the rows. Ribbons, bright scarves or other hair pieces could be used.

Follow the steps here and you can learn to cornrow. (Some people make designs — like hearts and initials.) Except for one step, cornrowing is almost like braiding.

Andrea's sister, Toni, makes the design here:

1. Part your hair and oil it at the scalp.
   The pattern that you part your hair in will be the pattern for the cornrows.
2. From one of the parted sections, hold 3 locks of hair in your hands.
3. Put the left lock and the middle lock in your left hand.
4. Put the right lock in your right hand.
5. First, take the middle lock up. Put it over the right lock.
   Do this each time you begin to cornrow.
   (In regular braiding you put the middle lock under instead of up.)
6. Keep braiding, putting the middle lock over each time.
   Pick up hair from the root and braid flat against the head.
7. Keep cornrowing until you finish 1 braid — and then twist the end so that it will stay together.

Barrettes

Here's a really simple way to make *Barrettes* for keeping your hair back.

You will need:
    some cardboard or poster
        board
    scissors
    marking pens
    shellac
    a stick from an ice cream bar

Here's what you do:
1. Cut something that looks like this:

2. Cut a hole out of the center like this:

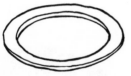

3. Draw a design with markers.
4. Shellac the rectangle and the stick.

Once the shellac is dry, you can pull your hair back and use your new homemade barrette.

Try it at home!

Rag Curls

ZOOMer Edith and her sister, Helen, make rag curls on each other.

You will need:
    scissors
    rags
    hair brush

Here's what you do:
1. Cut rags into long strips of about 5 x ½ inches. Depending on how many curls you want to make and how long your hair is, you'll need from 6 to 12 rags.
2. Wet brush and brush a small section of hair.

3. With the small section of hair, starting from the bottom, wrap the hair around the rag and roll the rag up all the way to the roots.
4. Tie the ends of the rag together tightly to secure the rag curl.
5. Do the rest of your hair in similar sections.
6. Leave the rags in overnight or until your hair dries.
7. Untie the rags and there are your curls!

TERRARIUM

Plants can live inside a *Terrarium* for a long time.

You will need:
- a fish tank (or any container made of plastic or glass)
- plastic wrap
- a "planting base" (use either well-fertilized soil or potting soil)
- sand and pebbles
- plants
- water

Here's what you do:

1. Make sure the container is waterproof. Line it with plastic wrap if necessary. Water must not seep out of the bottom or sides of the box.
2. Put the "planting base" in the bottom of the tank. This base consists of two layers: The sand and pebbles go on the bottom for drainage. (You may use different colors of sand which makes a design.) The soil goes on top of this.

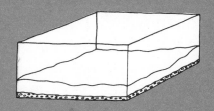

3. Landscape the soil if you want by putting slopes or hills in the tank. This makes the *Terrarium* more interesting and makes it easier to see all the plants.

4. Collect some small plants. Anything that grows in damp places will be fine. Moss collects on the ground near most trees and on lots of stones and rocks. Ferns grow wild almost everywhere.
   Be careful not to damage the roots when you dig up the plants.
5. After you arrange the plants the way you want them, sprinkle them with water. Do *not* pour water into the terrarium. You just need enough to make the soil damp.

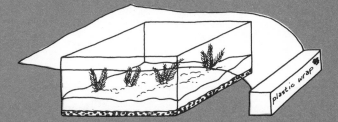

6. Cover the terrarium with the plastic wrap. Make sure it is very tight so no air will get in — and no water will get out.

You now have a tiny rain forest of your own. The water will condense on the plastic wrap, then fall down again to feed the plants. Check the soil every now and then, to make sure it's damp and wipe the plastic wrap if it gets too cloudy inside.

Don't worry if a plant dies. Some live longer than others. Take it out and put something new in its place.

ZOOMdoers: Donna Ferullo
Tim Brunelle
Weymouth, Massachusetts

Eggshell Garden

You will need:

- empty eggshells
- dye (food coloring will do)
- empty egg carton
- aluminum foil
- gravel
- dirt (soil)
- flower seeds

Here's what you do:

1. Use half an eggshell.
2. Dip eggshells in dye.
3. Line carton with aluminum foil.
4. Stand the shells in the egg carton.
5. Prick the bottom of each shell with a long needle — to make a pin hole to drain water.
6. Put a little gravel in the shells.
7. Now fill the shells with soil to about ½ inch from the top.
8. Put in 2 or 3 seeds.
9. Cover them with more soil.

10. Place your garden in a window.
11. Water every day.
12. Watch it grow!

— Bonnie Rosen, Jamaica, New York
Ellen Schindler, Silver Spring, Maryland

Crystal Garden

Caution: you should have adult supervision when you are working.

You will need:

- a shallow dish
- 3 or 4 pieces of charcoal (not briquettes)
- ¼ cup salt
- ¼ cup liquid blueing
- ¼ cup water
- 1 tablespoon of ammonia
- food coloring

Here's what you do:

1. Put the charcoal in the dish with rough edges facing up.
2. Mix the salt, blueing, water, and ammonia and pour the mixture over the charcoal.
3. Sprinkle different colors of food coloring over the charcoal. In about half an hour, it should start crystallizing and growing.

To keep your crystal garden blooming, just add a teaspoon of ammonia every week.

— Holly Helstern
Westchester, Illinois

Robin Easton of Geneva, New York, does the same thing with a brick. She writes that an old chipped one will do.

This is how to make a

Corn Garden
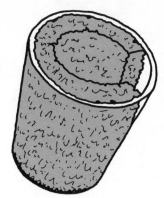

You will need:
  sponge
  glass
  corn kernels (popcorn)
  water
  soil
  container

1. Wedge the sponge in the glass.
2. Place kernels between wall of glass and sponge.
3. Put about an inch of water at the bottom of the glass.
4. As water evaporates, put more in until it's up to the same level. (Do not let corn fall when water is added.)
5. Leave in sunlight (but not direct sun).
6. In about ten days the corn will begin to sprout.
7. Plant the sprouts in a container filled with soil.
8. Make sure sprouts stick upward and watch how it grows.

— Liz Rafferty, Monroe, New York
Calvin Bradley, Smithville, Georgia

Enchilada Sauce

Here's a recipe we cowboys like out Arizona way. It has a Mexican origin and it's called *Enchilada Sauce*. You can put it on hot dogs, hamburgers, rice, noodles, and of course Enchiladas.

— John Smerecky
Peoria, Arizona

Note: If you're allowed to use the stove, go ahead. You may need to have an adult with you.

You will need:
  ⅓ cup vegetable oil
  1 clove finely chopped garlic
  3 tablespoons flour or cornmeal
  2 tablespoons red chili powder dissolved in a little hot water
  1 cup tomato sauce
  2 teaspoons salt
  large saucepan

Here's what you do:
1. Heat the oil and garlic in the pan over medium heat.
2. Add the flour or cornmeal and stir constantly until lightly browned.
3. Stir the dissolved chili powder into the mixture.
4. Continue stirring while adding the tomato sauce.
5. Add hot water to make the sauce as thick or thin as you wish.
6. Add salt.
7. Stir until it's hot.

It's good!

Edible Clay

peanut butter
dry, powdered milk
honey

1. Take equal amounts of peanut butter and dry, powdered milk, and put them in a mixing bowl.
2. Slowly add honey until the mixture is the thickness of clay.
   If it's too wet, add more dry milk. If it's too dry, add honey.
   For chocolate flavor, add cocoa.
3. Mold the mixture into anything you want. You may want to decorate it with raisins, nuts, seeds or candy.
4. When you finish your molding, you can eat it!

— Elena Kramnick
Peabody, Massachusetts

This is how Kelly Mullins of Gardiner, Maine, makes

Pumpkin Seeds

that are good to eat.

Here's what you do:
1. Pull the seeds out of the pumpkin and get the guck (pulp) off them.
2. Rinse in cold water.
3. Spread them on a cookie sheet and sprinkle them with salt.
4. Bake them for 5 minutes in a 500 degree oven.
5. Let them cool.
6. Eat!

Bean Sprouts

Caution: Do not use beans intended for outdoor planting. They may have a chemical coating that may be poisonous.

You will need:
- 1 one quart jar with wide mouth (a mayonnaise jar will do)
- ¼ cup of beans (many kinds of beans can be used, such as: lentils, alfalfa or peas.)
- water
- a piece of nylon netting (piece of old panty hose will do)
- a rubber band

Here 's what you do:
1. Put the beans in the jar and fill it with warm water.
2. Set it in a warm, dark corner of the kitchen.
3. Cover the top of the jar with nylon

netting and fasten it with a rubber band.

4. 24 hours later, dump the water out through the netting, leaving the beans in the jar.
5. Then, every day for the next 3 or 4 days, rinse the beans with fresh water and drain. Do it twice a day . . . once in the morning and once at night until the bean sprouts look like this:

6. Put the jar in the sun for the last day to make the sprouts green.
7. Then, rinse the beans to get rid of the hulls.

Store them in the refrigerator.
Eat them in sandwiches, salads or all by themselves.

Here's one bean recipe:

Chinese Sprout Salad

Put a *pound of bean sprouts* in a colander and pour boiling water over them. Rinse the sprouts with cold water. Make a dressing of *2 tablespoons soy sauce, 1 teaspoon peanut oil* and *1 teaspoon sugar*. Toss the salad in the dressing and chill.

— Missy Britton
Harwichport, Massachusetts

PEANUT BUTTER!

popcorn

You will need
- ⅓ cup butter or margarine
- ¼ cup peanut butter
- small pan
- 2 cups raisins
- 4 quarts popped corn (if you pop your own, it's less expensive)
- salt
- large bowl to hold everything

Here's what you do:
1. Melt the margarine and peanut butter in a small pan.
2. Stir in the raisins.
3. Put the popcorn in a bowl and pour the peanut butter mixture over it.
4. Toss lightly.
5. Put salt on it if you like.
6. Then eat it.

— Lorrain Steele
Volant, Pennsylvania

tasty toast topper

You will need:
- 3 tablespoons raisins
- 5 tablespoons peanut butter
- 2 tablespoons orange juice

Here's what you do:
1. Measure everything and put it all in a bowl or small cup.
2. Stir well.
3. Spread on hot toast.

— Nancy Kantorczyk
McKeesport, Pennsylvania

ants on a log

You will need *peanut butter, cleaned celery,* and *raisins.*

1. To make it all you do is put the peanut butter in the celery and put the raisins in the peanut butter. There you have it — ants on a log!
2. This is what it looks like:

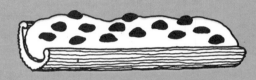

P.S. It's GOOD!

— Debra Spolski
Spokane, Washington

ZOOMspread

I have discovered a great food.

You will need:
- 1 banana
- 1 tablespoon of creamy peanut butter
- 2 tablespoons maple syrup
- 1 teaspoon honey

1. First you take the banana peel off.
2. Then you smash the banana in a bowl.
3. Then take the peanut butter and mix it in with the banana.
4. Put in the syrup and honey.

You've got your ZOOMspread to put on bread.

— Brenda Senne
Billings, Montana

Tortillas

This makes 16 tortillas. It's all right to use just half of everything if you only want 8 small tortillas.

5 cups flour
6 teaspoons baking powder
5 teaspoons salt
2 tablespoons lard
1½ cups warm water

To prepare the mixture:
1. Mix flour, baking powder, salt and lard in a large bowl.
2. After stirring ingredients add water and mix well. Make about 16 evenly-sized dough balls from this mixture.

3. With your hands work each ball of dough until it is as round and flat as you can make it. Then roll the dough with a rolling pin until it is as thin as possible.

To cook the tortillas:
Be sure to have an adult with you when you're using the stove!
1. Use a medium-low flame.
2. Grease a griddle or a frying pan and make sure it is warm.
3. Put each flat dough ball into the warmed pan and oil.

4. Flip the tortilla when it begins to brown and then cook the other side. (A tortilla takes only a few minutes to cook.)

When your tortillas are cooked you can fill them with anything you'd put in a sandwich. They're really good with chili, chicken, beans or beef. You could even use a salad or just peanut butter and jelly.

I live in Truchas, New Mexico. Truchas is big and it's pretty. Right outside my house I can see mountains. My family has lived in Truchas for many years. Most of the people who live here are Spanish.

Sometimes mother and I make tortillas. When we make them they are very pretty and round. But I can't make them as pretty and round as she can. When I make them they come out kind of funny shaped. And I can't make them as well.

You can fill tortillas with beans, with meat and with chili — and other things. You can even make a pizza out of a tortilla. We have them for breakfast and for lunch and for dinner. We eat tortillas all the time.

ZOOMdoer: Sylvia Trujillo
Truchas, New Mexico

HOMEMADE PRETZELS

You will need:
  1 bowl
  2 packets of dry yeast
  1½ cups warm water
  2 tablespoons sugar
  1 teaspoon salt
  4 cups flour
  waxed paper
  1 cookie sheet
  coarse salt
  1 egg, beaten
  pastry brush

Here's what you do:
1. Mix yeast and water in a bowl.
2. Add sugar and table salt.
3. Add flour. Mix.
4. Put the dough on some waxed paper on a table and knead it until it's smooth.
5. Cut off pieces and make them into shapes you like. Don't make them too thick or they'll be doughy. Try not to make them too thin or they'll be too brittle.
6. Place them on a cookie sheet.
7. Brush the pretzels with a beaten egg and then sprinkle them with the coarse salt. Cover all the top of the pretzel with egg.
8. Bake them at 425 degrees for 12 to 15 minutes or until they're golden brown.
9. Eat them!

— Susan, Margie and Anne Malloy
West Newton, Massachusetts

Cuban Cooking

In Cuba we used to eat this about twice a day. We don't really measure each ingredient. You just add it to taste.

— John de la Cruz
Mobile, Alabama

Ingredients:
  black beans
  1 pot
  1 pan
  chopped onions
  ½ green pepper
  salt
  pepper
  Spanish olive oil
  chopped garlic
  rice (not instant!)
  vegetable oil

To prepare black beans:
1. Place black beans into a pot of water overnight to let them get plump. Drain them.
2. Put plump beans into a pan and add a little water.
3. Add chopped onions, ½ green pepper, salt, pepper, olive oil and chopped garlic.
4. Let boil on medium heat for 3 hours. Set aside.

For rice, follow instructions on the package for right amount of water and rice. Cook according to directions. Serve the rice with the black beans on top of it.

Crayon monofold

My brother David taught me how to make a *Crayon Monofold*. And I am going to tell you how to make one too.

You will need:
  crayons
  scissors or a crayon sharpener (or something that will make shavings)
  paper
  newspaper
  an iron

1. Take a crayon and shave it (scrape it into very small pieces).

2. Put the pieces that you cut out on a piece of paper.

3. Fold the paper.

4. Fold the paper over again.
5. Put the paper between the newspaper. Then with a warm iron, go

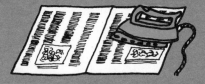

over the newspaper (keeping the iron in motion). The crayon will melt.
6. Open it up to see your creation.

— Deborah Todd
Glendale Heights, Illinois

Ann Hardy of New Orleans, Louisiana, also likes to do this, only she puts her crayon pieces between waxed paper.

Leaf Rubbing

Place a leaf on a flat surface so that the veins are facing up.
Place a sheet of paper over the leaf. Then take a crayon and color over the paper — hard, but not too hard.
When you are finished, remove the leaf.
That is all.

— Robin Bye
Westwego, Louisiana

Frank Gale of Peoria, Illinois, cuts his rubbings and mounts them on something else.

What kinds of rubbings do you make?

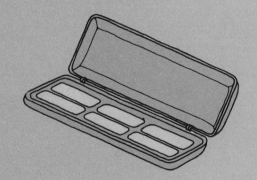

Crayon Resist Painting

You will need:
    a piece of paper for the background
    waxed paper or white crayon
    pencil with a dull point
    water-color paint

Here's what you do:
1. Put waxed paper over the background paper.
2. Bear down hard and draw a picture on the waxed paper with a pencil. *Or* with a white crayon draw a picture directly on the background paper.
3. Remove waxed paper.
4. With water colors paint over it lightly.

You've got it!

— Angilyn Cole
Indianapolis, Indiana

Your Own Mask

ZOOMdoers Frank Durgin, Kathy Rainwater, Rebecca and Vicky Sacks, and Pauline Kim of Cambridge, Massachusetts, made their masks.

To make your own mask you will need:
- a hard flat surface
- potter's clay (about 5 pounds)
- 1 bag of plaster of Paris (You won't need to use the whole bag.)
- gauze strips (It's easy to find surgical gauze in drug stores.)
- sand paper
- chisel or scissors
- string
- decorations (paint, feathers, beads, etc.)

Here's what you do:

1. Mold the clay on the board into the shape you want the mask to be. Try to make it just a little bigger than the size of your face.

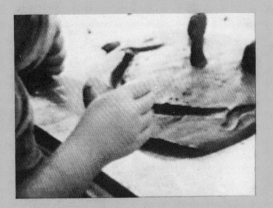

You can make the nose any size and shape you want.

You can make pointy ears, or a funny chin — and cheeks.

Remember that the mask will take on the shape of the clay.

2. Let the clay dry 8 to 10 hours or until it is dry when you touch it.

3. Mix the plaster of Paris with water.

The instructions are on the box. The solution should be liquid, but thick enough to coat the gauze.

4. Soak the gauze strips in the wet plaster, and cover the clay form with them.

Plaster dries quickly. If your supply begins to harden, you can add some water, or mix up another batch.

The clay should be completely covered by the gauze, with no cracks showing. Let the gauze strips dry for about 15 to 30 minutes, or until it feels dry all over when you touch it. (Before it dries completely, you can put some feathers or beads in it. But don't paint the mask yet!)

5. The plaster mask should separate from the clay as it dries. If it doesn't, carefully pry it off the form around the edges.

6. Smooth the front and edges of the mask with sand paper and/or a chisel. You can also cut out eyes, a nose and a mouth with the chisel or scissors.

7. Cut one hole on each side where you put strings to hold the mask on your head.

8. Decorate the mask with paint, beads or whatever else you want to use.

9. Tie strings through the side holes and wear your mask!

TILE MOSAIC

ZOOMdoers: Mark Roden
Linda Kelleher
Jimmy Lawlor
Jeanne McManus
Quincy, Massachusetts

You will need:

- plywood board (or any hard even surface that's the right size for your design)
- waxed paper
- self-hardening clay
- rolling pin
- 2 thick-edged rulers
- a dull knife
- cookie sheet (optional)
- newspaper
- paint (liquid enamel is fine even though it takes a long time to dry)
- turpentine
- glue (any household kind)
- clear varnish (optional)

Here's what you do:

1. Sketch your design on your board for a guideline. You may want to first try some ideas with pencil and paper. Decide on a color arrangement, and avoid a design that needs shading.
2. Cover the surface you're going to work on with waxed paper so the clay won't stick. You can tape the waxed paper down so it won't slip.
3. Pound your clay until it's soft enough to work easily with your hands.
4. Flatten the clay out and cover with a sheet of waxed paper.
5. Use a rolling pin over the waxed paper and roll the clay until it's thin.

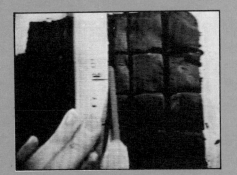

Use the rulers on each side to measure and make sure it's the same thickness. When you're finished the clay should be ¼ inch thick and have an even surface.

6. Cut the clay into squares. Cut vertical strips first. Then cut across to make squares. Cut some squares in halves,

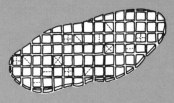

quarters and triangles for tiles to fit the small areas of the design.

7. Let the clay dry overnight or dry it quickly by putting it on a cookie sheet in a 300 degree oven for 30 minutes.
8. To make sure you have enough tiles, lay them out on your board. Leave ⅛ inch space between every tile — on all sides.
9. Spread out the newspaper.
10. Arrange the tiles for each color in separate piles on the newspaper.
11. Paint your separate groups of tiles the colors you chose. Only one side of each tile should be painted — a little goes a long way! (Liquid enamel should dry overnight.)
12. Leave the board plain.

13. When the paint is dry, glue each tile to the board while using your pencil design as a guide.
14. Put the mosaic aside overnight so that the glue dries and sets the tiles in place.
15. If you want the tiles to have a shiny finish, apply a coat of clear varnish.
16. A frame can be added, but it's not necessary.

Your mosaic is ready to hang on a wall or to be made into a table!

Clay Mobiles

You will need:
- food coloring (about 20 drops)
- 1½ cups water
- 4 cups flour
- 1 cup salt
- a rolling pin
- a pencil
- a cookie sheet
- tinfoil
- some string

This recipe makes enough for a few mobiles, so it you're only making one, use half the amount of each ingredient. Or invite some of your friends to help and make the whole recipe. This clay can be saved for a while in a plastic bag, but be sure not to forget it. Use it up as soon as you can because it does dry out.

If you want to paint the finished pieces, you can use acrylic paints after the pieces have cooled. Do not eat!

Here's what you do:
1. Mix the food coloring into the water. It should make a good deep color.
2. Put the flour, salt, and colored water together in a big bowl. Mix.
3. The dough should be a little stiff, but if it is too dry you can add a little water — a few drops at a time. Be careful! If you add too much water, it won't work.
4. After the dough is mixed really well, roll it out with a rolling pin on an

opened paper bag or waxed paper. Stop rolling before the dough gets too thin.

5. Make whatever shapes you'd like to use. Cut out the shapes. Make them large enough to leave room for a hole in each one so that a string can be used for hanging. *Or* you can build three-dimensional pieces with your hands instead of making flat pieces.

Smaller and thinner things take less than an hour. It's all right to peek along the way. Your finished piece should be hard to the touch when you take it out of the oven.

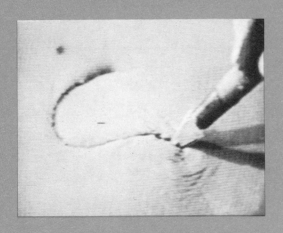

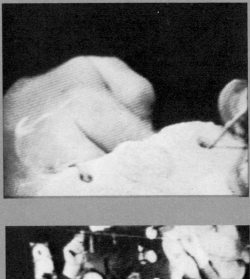

6. Use the point of a pencil or pen to make a hole in each shape.
7. Line a cookie sheet with tinfoil.
8. Place each piece carefully onto the cookie sheet. (They shouldn't be too close to one another.)
9. Bake the pieces in a 250 degree oven for about an hour.

10. When the pieces are cool, insert strings and hang them to make a mobile.

— Scott McDonald
Robert Trevison
South Boston, Massachusetts

You will need:
    2 empty tin cans of the same size (tall
        juice cans are good)
    heavy string or cord (2 pieces about as
        tall as you are)
    a can opener
    scissors

Here's what you do:
1. Remove one end of each can.
2. Punch two holes in the closed end of
   each can.

3. Thread the string or cord through one
   hole and up the other in each can.
4. Hold the two ends in your hand.

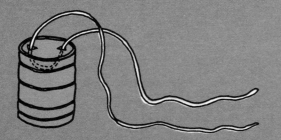

5. Stand on top of the tin cans and hold
   onto the strings tightly.
6. Walk!

— Robin Barnes
Brooklyn, New York

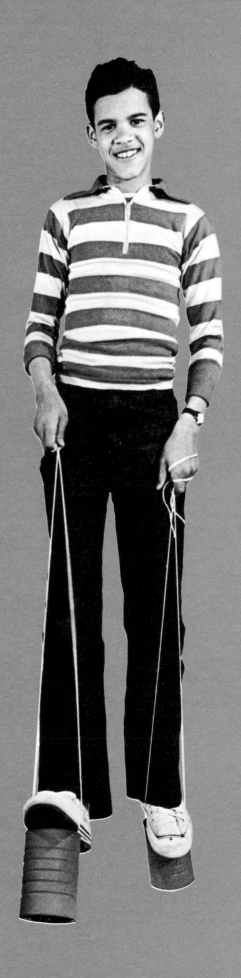

Straw Weaving

I know you'll have fun doing this. You can make belts, bracelets and chokers by *Straw Weaving.*

You will need:
- 1 pair of scissors
- 1 ball of yarn or string (string could be difficult)
- 3 plastic drinking straws

Here's what you do:
1. Cut 3 pieces of yarn about 27 inches long for a necklace or a belt. If you're guessing how much you need, measure at least 18 extra inches longer than the finished weaving should be.
2. Tie lots of knots in one end of each length of yarn (or string) and then tape the end of yarn to the straws so that it won't slip back through the straw.
3. Pull the yarn through the straws.
4. Tie the 3 pieces of yarn together at the end without the knots with a short piece of string.
   Here is what it should look like:

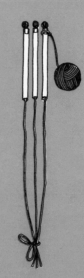

5. Tie the end of your yarn ball onto an outer straw. Then weave the yarn over and under the straws.

When the straws are covered, push your weaving down onto the lengths of yarn.

When it's as long as you want it, push all the weaving down onto the pieces of yarn and release the straws.
6. Tie knots at the ends so the weaving won't come out.

It's finished!
If you want to do a wider weaving, use 4 or 5 straws.

— Betsy Duncan
Rumson, New Jersey

TREE

You need something to hang the loom from.

You can use
  a low branch on a tree
  a swing set
or even
  a clothesline that is stretched really tight.

When you've decided what you're going to use, get your materials together.

You will need:
  lots of heavy string
  2 strong sticks (about 4 feet long)
  2 large rocks
  weaving material (You can use all sorts of things — yarn, ribbon, little sticks, crumpled foil — almost anything!)

Here's what you do to build the loom:
1. Cut 2 pieces of heavy string — each about 2 feet longer than the distance from the branch (or whatever you are using) to the ground. Tie each piece around the branch about 2 feet apart.
2. Now hold 1 of the sticks horizontally about 2 feet below the branch and tie the 2 pieces of string around it.
3. Then hang the second stick about 3 or 4 feet under the first stick tying the string in the same way.
4. Then put the 2 heavy rocks on the ground under each string and tie what string is left

LOOM

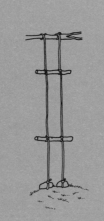

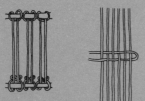

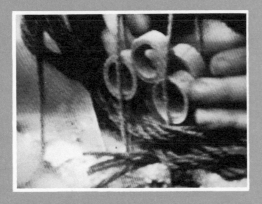

around both of them.

All the strings should be tight all the way down. It will look something like the picture at left.

To weave:

1. Cut about 24 pieces of heavy string, each about 8 feet long.

2. Fold each string in two and put the loop over the top stick. Then thread the two ends of the string through the loop and tie the two loose ends tightly to the stick below.

   Space each string along the sticks about an inch apart. These strings are called the "warp."

3. Whatever material you are weaving with is called the "weft." The weft goes across the warp strings from side to side, starting at the bottom.

   If you want to remove your finished weaving from the loom, it is important to start far enough from the bottom knot so that you could tie a knot with each end piece of warp.

4. Start at the bottom, put the weft first *over* and then under the warp strings, one or two at a time. Any way is fine as long as it stays.

5. The next weft should go first *under*, then over the warp strings.

   Keep going. You can either pack the wefts tightly together or leave them loose. Just make sure that everything is secure.

6. If you're going to use your weaving as an indoor hanging, a rug or a table decoration, cut it off the tree and knot each end string so that your weaving will hold together.

— Lisa and David Cohen
Weston, Massachusetts

Rag Tapestry

This could be a good group project. ZOOM-doers from Roxbury, Massachusetts, Laura and Lisa Boraks, Pamela Fuller, Elizabeth Cole, Barry Gordon and Joe Barry had a good time making theirs.

You will need:
    paper for drawing
    tracing paper
    charcoal or chalk
    burlap or monk's cloth
    black magic marker
    needle with a large eye
    heavy thread or string
    stretcher (an old picture frame that is at least 14 x 20 inches will do)
    scissors
    wool, knit or cloth rags, material or yarn
    a shuttle hook (found in most hobby stores) or a rug punch (If you use a rug punch, you must use yarn instead of rags.)
    crochet hook

Here's what you do:
1. Draw a simple design on the drawing paper. Make sure it is 1½ inches smaller than the frame.
2. Using tracing paper and either chalk or charcoal, trace over the design you have just drawn.
3. Now flip the tracing over onto burlap and rub the tracing so that the design prints onto the burlap.
4. After the design has rubbed off onto the burlap, trace over it with magic marker.

This is the back of your tapestry. Start all the work with the shuttle hook on this side of the burlap.

5. Now, with the needle and heavy thread or string, stitch the burlap very tightly onto the frame or the stretcher.

6. Cut your wool or cloth into long ¼ inch wide strips with scissors.

7. Sort these strips into plastic bags according to color.

8. Thread your shuttle hook or rug punch with your strips of material or yarn (one at a time).

9. If you use a shuttle hook, grip the handles and slide them back and forth, while punching the burlap and leaving loops of the material.

10. Fill in your design using your different colored strips. Leave no spaces unfilled. You might outline the outside of your design in a darker color cloth or wool and then fill in the designs with colors.

11. Use the crochet hook to pull all ends to the front of your design.

12. Snip the front of the design so that all ends are even.

Now you can:

1. Leave the rag tapestry on the frame and use it as is (if it has become too loose just tighten it up) *or*

2. Cut it off the frame and hem it to make a wall hanging *or*

3. Make a pillow by cutting another piece of fabric to sew on for a back.

This is called a

SITUPON

All you will need is:
newspaper
scissors
tape

Here's what you do:
1. First, take a sheet of newspaper and fold it in half like a book. Fold it over again.
2. Then fold it again; it should be about an inch and a half wide.
3. Make about 20 such strips. (You can make more depending upon how large you want your *Situpon* to be.)
4. Place 10 or 11 of the strips of paper next to each other so they line up vertically.
5. Then take another strip and begin weaving it horizontally into the strips about an inch from the top.
6. Do the same with 9 other strips so it looks like the picture.
   Make sure that the weaving is tight!
   You will have 10 back and forth strips which alternate under, over, under, over.
7. Then tape the ends down.

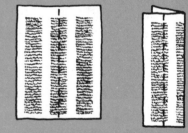
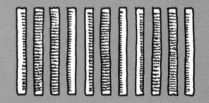

— Jane Gemein
Chicago, Illinois

Get
ready...

now...

sit upon it!

answers

cups puzzle

First turn over cups A and B.
Next turn over cups A and C.
Then turn over cups A and B.

ice cube phenomenon

Pour a little salt on ice before you lift it up.

ZOOMthanks

Adults who helped with ZOOMdos:

Curt Chapin
Stewart T. Coffin
Linda Hatch Dow
Anita Fisk
Cynthia Guertin
Toni Federico-Acker
Kay Hudgins
Trintje Jansen
Margda Johnson
Rita Killam
Adrienne Lowenthal
Jo Madden

John Mahoney
Karen Foote Richards
Marty Richardson
Bernard Pendleton
Richard Porteus
Bernard Tole
Mary Toomey
Camille Turner
Barbro Ulander
Ann Wiseman
Staff of the American School
    for the Deaf

And special thanks to the ZOOMail people who open as many as 20,000 letters a week.

ZOOMstaff 1974–1975:

Executive Producer	Austin Hoyt
Studio Producer	Ron Blau
Studio Directors	D. Keith Carlson
	Bruce Shah
Film Producers	Mary Benjamin Blau
	Janet Weaver
Unit Manager	Nancy Troland
Associate Producers	Kate Taylor
	Rebecca Eaton
Contributions Editor	Joanne Grady
Music Director	Newton Wayland
Musical Staging	Billy Wilson
	Millard Hurley
Research Coordinator	Bernice Chesler
Mail Coordinator	Jo Madden
Post Production Supervisor	Neil Weisbrod
Assistant Unit Manager	Patricia Gregson
Production Assistants	Tony Davis
	Susie Dangel
Program Assistant	Janet Krause

index